the
humming
✤f
Numbers

the humming of Numbers

JONI SENSEL

Henry Holt and Company
New York

Henry Holt and Company, LLC
Publishers since 1866
175 Fifth Avenue
New York, New York 10010
www.HenryHoltKids.com

Library of Congress Cataloging-in-Publication Data
Sensel, Joni.
The humming of numbers / Joni Sensel.—1st ed.
p.   cm.
Summary: Aiden, a novice about to take monastic vows in tenth-century
Ireland, meets Lana, a girl who understands his ability to hear the sounds of
numbers humming from all living things, and just as he is beginning to
question his religious calling, the two of them are thrown together in a mission
to save their village from invading Vikings.
ISBN-13: 978-0-8050-8327-9 / ISBN-10: 0-8050-8327-8
[1. Monastic and religious life—Fiction.   2. Witches—Fiction.   3. Vikings—
Fiction.   4. Ireland—History—To 1172—Fiction.]   I. Title.
PZ7.S4784Hu 2008   [Fic]—dc22   2007027569

First Edition—2008
Book designed by Laurent Linn
Printed in the United States of America on acid-free paper. ∞

1   3   5   7   9   10   8   6   4   2

For Tom, who helped me to hear it again

the humming ❧f Numbers

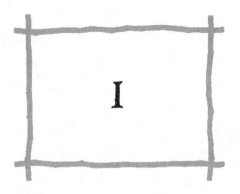

I

Lana Nicarbith hummed of the number eleven. The sound caught Aidan's attention as he swept the path near the abbey's front gate. He stared, open-mouthed, while Lord Donagh dragged the girl through the entry, past Aidan's poised broom, and inside. Plenty of people filled Aidan's ears with the chiming of four or seven or nine, and many of his brothers in the order purred softly of six. Never in his seventeen years, though, had Aidan O'Kirin met anyone endowed with the energy of a number higher than ten. He'd seen Lana before, but only from a distance—too far to hear the eleven that wafted from her now like fragrance from a flower.

Aidan followed. He noted the hand clamped on her arm and wondered why the ruler of eight clans had hauled his bastard daughter to the monks. His own footsteps quickened, along with his pulse. He risked a chiding if the abbot saw him being nosy, but the birch broom in his work-calloused hands gave him a meager excuse. He trailed a few paces behind Donagh and the slender ginger-haired girl. They angled through the yard toward the abbot's quarters, which sat near the gate on the sunny side of the stone chapel.

Clearly not happy to be there, the eleven girl stamped her bare feet and struggled and screeched.

"Stop squawking," Donagh ordered, yanking her forward. Fury and embarrassment glowed from his face. "This is a holy place."

"Not to me," she retorted, her head whipping around. Her eyes struck Aidan. Impaled by their blue fire, he did not drop his regard as would have been proper. She went stiff. Her protests fell silent. The humming eleven, if anything, grew louder.

Aidan had realized long ago that he alone heard the numbers humming from people and things. To him, the mathematical tones were as natural as colors or smells, just one more detail to notice and rather more pleasant than a whiff of dung or sour breath. His attempts to discuss it as a small boy, however, had failed. Nobody understood when he tried to explain. He'd been humored, at best, and more often had met with bewildered irritation. While still young, he'd grasped the truth: Others heard birdsong, windsong, human speech. But nobody else heard the more subtle buzzing that he did. The music of numbers otherwise fell on deaf ears.

So the girl staring back at him now, the one whose skin whispered eleven, could not have been startled for the same reason he had been. She should have been embarrassed, caught acting so wildly, yet her face spoke plainly of some disappointment. It seemed to be aimed straight at Aidan. Wondering why, he raised his eyebrows in silent inquiry. She scowled. After a long, frowning look, with her neck craned to keep him in view, she stopped resisting completely and turned to follow sullenly behind her captor. The flash of silent communion between her and Aidan had somehow proved more persuasive than the lord's command or rough handling.

They approached the abbot's thatched house. Donagh rapped on the door, which opened to admit them. Nobody bothered to close it behind them. Aidan halted to perform some halfhearted sweeping in case the abbot reemerged with the visitors in tow. Fixing his brown eyes on the already-smooth ground, he let a swath of his dark hair partly hide his narrow face.

When the doorway remained empty, the young monk-in-training slipped nearer. His feet, still bare in the autumn sunshine, padded soundlessly on the earth. They faltered near a stone bench tucked under the abbot's thatched eaves. Aidan didn't dare venture closer. He was supposed to be sweeping the path near the gate and meditating on cleanliness and purity before the noon prayers. It would be impossible to even pretend obedience if he went any farther. Poking his broom at a dead leaf under the bench, he tried to quiet his breath, the better to eavesdrop.

"She was alongside the pilgrims' route," Lord Donagh was saying. "Selling these. Or trying to." Aidan's ears caught the clatter of wood tumbling across the table.

"Pilgrims are beset by evil at every turn," sighed Abbot Bartley. The abbey was an attraction along the popular Saint Nevin's Way, and brigands and thieves knew it well. Many a pilgrim arrived empty-handed or beaten, giving the monks ample chance to practice hospitality and compassion.

The girl in the abbot's dim chamber apparently had no interest in compassion. "If they're foolish enough to believe that their sins can be wiped away just by—"

Her voice was interrupted by what sounded like a slap. Aidan had never met Donagh directly, but he'd grown up in the shadow of the lord's fist. It fell unevenly across Donagh's domain. Wealthy enough to sneer at the fines imposed for his own misdeeds, the lord invoked the law when it pleased him and scoffed when it did not. Aidan had long ago pegged the man as an eight, although less kind than most and even more unpredictable.

"Shut your mouth, or I'll see that shame shuts it for

you," Lord Donagh growled to the girl. "Since you can't pay the restitution accorded your crime, I'm tempted to chain you in the stocks and let pilgrims loose their spittle on you. Your mother's pleading is the only reason you're not there already."

Aidan's slender artisan's fingers tightened on his broom handle. He'd seen dishonored men in the stocks, with their ankles locked in place, unable to dodge any foul thing pitched their way. And spittle was hardly the worst thing that flew. The thought of the girl's pretty face splattered with rotten fruit or manure made him cringe.

The threat frightened her as well, evidently.

"Forgive me, Rí," she murmured, using the traditional title that acknowledged his rank. She knew better than to call him Father, Aidan noted, even though that's who he was. Unlike some noblemen, who boasted the count of their illegitimate children, Donagh preferred to ignore them. Aidan reflected how difficult it must have been for her to grow up amid so much pretense and gossip.

"But why have you brought her to me, lordship, if I may ask?" The abbot sounded dismayed. Some cousin of the lord, the two-ish fellow did not much like surprises.

His ears straining, Aidan risked moving closer.

"Put her to work in the kitchen or fields" came the reply. "She needs a dose of humility. Perhaps hard work and the Holy Spirit may cleanse her of sinful ways."

"But, Lord Donagh, surely a convent would be—"

"Don't be ridiculous. She's not worth the cost of entry at Saint Brigid's, not to mention the trip. Besides, we've had word of Norsemen on the move."

"Nearby, my lord?" Bartley squeaked. A Viking raid might bring fleeing farmers into the monastery's already bustling enclosure. The defensive ramparts could help repel raiders while the holy bones of the saint offered even more potent protection.

"Not that I've heard. But travel is out of the question. You have a wife here yourself, do you not? As does Father Niall."

"Yes, but—"

"She can be confined here, then. She's not handsome enough to threaten any chastity vows."

The abbey rules forbade argument, and besides, Aidan could hardly speak up from outside, but contrary thoughts crossed his mind. The lord must have meant mostly to brush off objections.

"If she causes you trouble," Donagh continued, "more extreme measures will be necessary."

"No, please," came the girl's voice, even softer than before. "Please don't chain me or send me to nuns far away."

"But, your lordship—"

"As a favor to me, Bartley. I will express my gratitude to you and Saint Nevin on Sunday. With silver."

"As you wish, then," the abbot sighed. Donagh's vassals griped about his rents and his temper, but few who tilled his lands or depended on his favor would dare speak against him. The abbot proved no exception. "We will try."

Aidan busied himself with his broom as Lord Donagh took his farewell. The lord emerged abruptly over the threshold with a scowl. Accustomed to the presence of both servants and monks, he did not give the thin, sharp-faced novice so much as a glance.

The stamping footsteps retreated toward the gate.

"Peddling false relics is a serious sin," Abbot Bartley said after a moment of silence.

"How do you know they're false?" the girl asked. Spirit had returned to her voice.

"Even we don't have fragments of the True Cross," he scoffed.

"Exactly," she said. "So you don't know what it looks like, do you? Touch it. 'Tis not oak or elm or alder, certainly. So this *could* be the wood of the Cross, couldn't it?"

Aidan grinned despite the sober accusation against the girl.

"Broken rake handle, more likely," the abbot said. "How would a lowly girl like you possess a relic like that?"

"A tree sprite told me where to dig near the base of its tree," she replied.

Aidan's eyebrows shot up. He'd heard a few people

claim to commune with the Otherworld, but her whirring eleven gave her words weight. They also troubled his heart.

Numbers had hummed to Aidan his entire life. By his twelfth year, however, when his father had first suggested the monastery, Aidan had stopped mentioning them to others. After a few winters of study, the thoughtful young loner had decided his awareness of numbers must be the whisper of God, a gift delivered to him and not anyone else. He had embraced the idea of joining the monks, and not only because his three older brothers would claim all of his father's cattle and pigs. Saints often heard voices, after all. Hearing the humming of numbers was not so different. Or so Aidan hoped.

Not long after formally becoming a novice last fall, he had cautiously brought up the subject with his mentor. Brother Eamon's reaction had dispelled Aidan's sense of privilege, planting a fear in its place: A whisper that nobody else heard might come not from God but from demons.

That same dread rose again now at the new arrival's claim.

"Enough lies, young charlatan," Bartley told the girl in his chamber. The abbot obviously held no belief in tree sprites and no fear of demons. "You would have done better to confess your sin. But I trust that a day of fasting will strengthen your soul."

"He said kitchen work," she protested, as more footsteps sounded. Feet scuffled as if their owner were dragged.

"There will be grain enough to grind on the morrow. Until then, my lamb, you can reflect."

"Wait! My wood—"

"You won't need it."

They were about to emerge. Aidan realized that he should have moved away sooner. Now he would almost surely be spotted and censured.

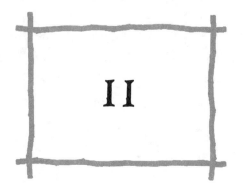

II

Frozen in indecision, Aidan resisted the urge to flee. He could duck 'round the nearest corner, but that would not be far enough to keep him out of sight for more than a few seconds, and the pounding of running feet in a monastery would betray him even more quickly than a glimpse of his form. The wisest course was to drop to his knees and beg forgiveness even as the abbot emerged and spied him there.

Instead Aidan dove under the wide stone bench. His shoulders and spine cracked painfully against the stone. Folding tight, he drew up his lanky legs, dragged the broom in behind him, and was obscured by the bench's shadow as well as its thick stone feet. The tight space reminded him sharply that such antics were better left to boys half his age. Too late; the abbot's leather slippers stepped over the sill. Aidan held his breath.

Two pairs of feet hurried by without hesitation. As they vanished around a corner, gratitude washed over Aidan.

Then the gravity of what he'd just done squeezed his chest. He wasn't afraid of punishment so much as a blot on his reputation. Aidan wanted badly to serve in the scriptorium, and he'd only recently been allowed to scrape calfskin to help make the vellum pages. It was hard work, and his hands were always sore, but even that taste of the scribes' duties thrilled him. The inks he'd glimpsed didn't just hum but actually shouted at him, numbers in pure liquid form. He couldn't wait to feel a goose quill balanced in his own fingers, to draw it across a page leaving a graceful mark. No other worship could compare to the honor of copying beauty and wisdom in red and green ink, lapis lazuli, and fine dabs of gold.

A novice who shirked his duties to hide under benches, however, would never touch quills or inks, let alone the great books. He lay in the dirt and shadows, his heart pumping, until well after the footsteps had faded. He felt trapped by the notion that someone would see him crawling out from under the bench.

The realization that his brethren would soon pass by on their way to midday prayers finally drove him out. Seeing no one in the yard, he took a deep breath, slid sideways, and scrambled to his feet.

"Napping, Brother Aidan?"

Aidan whirled. A hawk-faced old monk stood in the abbot's doorway, a thin smile on his lips.

The smooth voice continued. "Or just hearing the spiders' confessions before you sweep them away?"

Sickened, Aidan fumbled for words. It had never occurred to him that anyone else might have been with the abbot when Lord Donagh had entered. He should have heeded his instinct to wait. Having been both a fool and a weakling, now he'd reap the results: Brother Nathan ran the scriptorium.

Knowing it was too late, Aidan dropped to one knee. His face burned. "Forgive me, Brother Nathan. I saw them arrive, and I gave in to my curiosity."

"Curiosity is not a sin that I am aware of," said Nathan. "Deception, however . . ." He paused. The air was filled only with the purr of Brother Nathan's elegant but uncompromising nine.

Realizing he'd heard that number faintly from under the bench but had simply ignored it, Aidan forced himself to ask, "How should I atone for my failure?" He expected an order to confess to the abbot as well as to Brother Eamon. No doubt he'd be assigned some unpleasant task to help cleanse his soul.

When he got no response, Aidan gulped against the lump in his throat. He felt his dreams shriveling. "Please guide me," he pleaded, keeping his gaze on the older monk's feet. Certain Brother Nathan was aware of his hopes, he added, "I want to be worthy of your work. How can I become more deserving?"

"Sweep," said Brother Nathan. "That is what brooms are best suited for. Or sit on the bench, which is better suited for that than lying beneath." He stepped around Aidan to leave.

Aidan leaned on his broom, shuddering in relief. Brother Nathan was letting him off with great kindness and humor.

The departing monk added a few words over his shoulder. "When I think you are suited to copying Holy Scripture," he said, "I will let you know."

To Aidan it sounded as though he could sooner expect the return of the Messiah. That, if it took place in the year 1000 as most everyone guessed, was still some fourscore years away. Certainly Aidan would not live to see it. The young monk slowly rose back to both feet, wishing he'd been anywhere else when the abbey's troublesome new guest had arrived.

Trouble had avoided him neatly until then, with just one exception. Having performed well as a student, mastering Latin and memorizing all 150 Psalms, Aidan had eagerly donned the robe of a novice when it had been offered at last. The monks' scratchy gray wool muttered of twenty-one against his skin. He had stopped hearing it soon enough. Like the scents in a field of flowers, numbers murmured in his ears so continually that they faded unless he tried to hear them—or was startled, as he had been by Lana.

Once cloaked in a monk's robe, however, Aidan had felt obligated to mention the humming of numbers to Brother Eamon. In trying to explain, he had made the mistake of saying that many of his fellow monks brought the number six to his mind. A horrified look had crossed Brother Eamon's face. The senior monk fretted that Aidan might be bewitched by the Number of the Beast recorded in Saint John's Revelation. He'd assigned Aidan three full days of solitary prayer to inspect his heart. The novice obeyed without protest. To himself, though, Aidan scoffed. Whether the Beast's number was 666 or 616 remained a matter of far-off church debate, according to the abbot, but how anyone could fear any combination of sixes, Aidan didn't know. Sixes were soft-spoken, slow-moving, and kind. Only long contemplation had helped him understand that such deception might be the Beast's secret.

The Beast crossed Aidan's mind now as he recalled the piercing look the girl had given him in the yard. Both her squeals and her wild struggle against the lord's grip could have been caused by a demon. Aidan had a hard time believing that demons could enter through a person's nostrils or ears. If she did have a monster inside her, however, growling through her eleven, perhaps Brother Eamon was right. Perhaps the numbers he heard came from somewhere much darker than heaven.

More troubling yet, any demon inside her may have peeked out through her blue eyes and spied him there listening. Certainly something in her had taken notice when their gazes had locked.

Aidan shoved that fear from his heart, loath to believe that the humming of numbers, as natural to him as the sunshine and considerably more dependable, could be powered by evil. No dark force could make *everyone* hum.

He could not sweep thoughts of the eleven girl so easily from his mind. Curiosity swelled in him, and after the noon prayers he found an excuse to pass through the guesthouse. Since novices were often expected to tend to guests' needs, they were permitted to come and go freely from that building. The new arrival was not there, not even in the portion reserved for the poorest pilgrims. Aidan began to think the abbot may have taken her outside the compound after all. Perhaps she'd been lodged with servants in one of the cottages huddled near the abbey's gates.

Then, late that afternoon, he spotted pale, feminine fingers draped out of a narrow slot in a stone wall facing the rose garden. She'd been locked in a penitent's cell, the same one where Aidan once had been instructed to pray about numbers and 666. Her fingers reached and dawdled in the ventilation gap as if they, at least, would be free in the waning sunlight.

Fortunately for Aidan, the abbey's elders were accustomed to seeing novices weeding the roses. So with a few minutes to spare before Vespers, he crouched in the soft dirt and began weeding his way toward the languishing fingers.

Aidan liked to weed. Plucking unwanted sprouts from among the holiest flowers of Christ was honorable work. In Aidan's first week as a novice, Brother Eamon had explained how weeding mimicked the plucking of sin, bit by bit, from one's soul. Aidan sometimes meditated on that idea as he worked, but mostly he enjoyed the colors, the scents, and the numbers of the roses and of each tiny weed. In removing the intruders, he paid special attention to the veins and shapes of their leaves. When he finally became a scribe, he would draw beautiful leaves and vines into the borders of manuscripts he illuminated.

"Oh! You. Halloo there."

Aidan started, having almost forgotten that he wasn't just weeding. From his crouch he could see that deep in the recess where her fingers had stretched, the girl's round cheek now pressed to the slit. One brilliant blue eye gazed out at him. Her eleven-ness struck him again, trilling, and he dismissed the concern that had crept over him earlier. That sound couldn't possibly be demonic. It was too radiant, too distilled, and now he thought he understood a bit more. She wasn't a thief, exactly, but Aidan guessed that the clever seven he'd heard so often from thieves had combined with her girlish four-ness to catapult her past nine and all the way to that intriguing, enticing eleven.

"You're young, for a monk," she said. "You can't be much older than I am."

"I haven't taken my final vows yet," Aidan murmured. "I'm still just a novice." He wasn't so young, either; the abbey's thirteen-year-old monk was constantly held up as an example. Four years older, Aidan often felt half as learned or pious—or obedient. Reflexively, he glanced over his shoulder to make sure no one was watching.

"Are you scared you'll get in trouble if you talk to me?" A taunt lurked in her voice.

He scowled. "Not scared," he said, but he kept his voice very low.

She sighed. Her feisty tone vanished. "You will, won't you?"

He was almost certain the answer was yes. Idle chatting was frowned upon. Modest and useful speech was permitted until the last evening prayers, but those locked in the penitent cells were left wholly to reflection. Of course, this girl was no monk, so perhaps none of the usual rules applied. Aidan knew that to be wishful thinking, but it allowed him to take a risk that he could not resist.

"You're supposed to be mortifying your flesh and con-templating your sins," he whispered, hunkering closer so his voice wouldn't drift beyond the roses.

"My flesh *is* mortified," she said. "I'm cold and starving and stuck here in the dark. Isn't that enough?"

Aidan didn't bother to mention the small whip in that cell for penitents to punish themselves with. He hadn't beaten himself with it, either. She didn't wait for an answer anyway.

"Never mind that," she said. "What's your name?"

Afraid he was seeding weeds into his soul instead of plucking them out but unable to stop himself, he told her.

"O'Kirin?" she asked. "I know your sister. How odd I've never met you before."

"I've been here for most of the last five years," he explained. "But I've seen you on feast days. When you noticed me in the yard, I thought maybe you knew me. You looked—"

"No," she said, so hastily that Aidan wondered why she denied it. "I'm Lana," she continued quickly. "I live down-river near the quarry with my mother."

"I know," he replied. "One of Lord Donagh's daughters."

Even through the narrow slot, her surprise showed. "How did you know he's my father?" she asked, her voice low.

"Everyone knows," Aidan said, with a shrug. "People like to talk about highborn folk, and they especially like to gossip about their bastards. Makes 'em more like the rest of us."

After a pained silence, she said, " 'Natural child' is a kinder way to say it."

"What's unkind about bastard? 'Tis the truth." Wishing he could see more of her face, he added, "Besides, it was hardly your fault."

"He acts like it was," she said softly. "And so does most everyone else."

"Donagh can bed any woman he wants, whether the rest of us like it or not." Aidan tried to keep the bitterness out of his voice. His eldest brother, wed to a beautiful wife, had learned this hard lesson firsthand. Relieved it had been only once, those who knew of the affront never questioned whether Liam's young son was actually his. The honor-price Donagh had paid for that trespass had partly funded Aidan's entrance to the monastery, however, so he, at least, could not forget it. The injustice weighed on his own conscience and silently rankled his heart.

"But 'tis harder to ignore when fatherless children are born of it," he added, feeling a secret bond with Lana. "You're a reminder. People only scowl at you because they don't dare scowl at him. Perhaps they should." Abruptly realizing that a monk should not speak so frankly, he checked over his shoulder again before finishing lamely, "After all, adultery is a sin."

"Monks think everything is a sin," she grumbled. "If I'm so evil, why are you talking to me?"

"I never said you were evil," he protested, though he'd considered exactly that notion earlier. He didn't reply to the second part of her question. He wanted to tell her she was the only eleven he'd ever met, but after Brother Eamon's reaction, he'd learned to keep his mouth shut about numbers.

"I wish I was home." Sighing, she drew back from the slot in the wall.

With a pang of sympathy, Aidan said softly, "Sounds to me as though you live here now, at least for a while. 'Tis not so bad. There's usually plenty of food, and we're safe from clan raids and—"

Just then a bell clanged.

"Time for Vespers," he said, brushing dirt from his fingers. "I have to go."

"Wait," she pleaded. "I can't see the sky, so I won't see the moon or the stars. When the sun's gone, it will be black in here. And I'm afraid of things in the dark. Don't you have any candles to burn?"

The novices' dormitory had a lamp that burned most of the night, but Aidan knew she would have no such luxury. "Go to sleep now, and you won't notice," he suggested.

She didn't answer. He could feel her fear seep out through the slit in the wall. Fear always droned of the number one, and hers was tinny and bleak. The novice rubbed his palms against the coarse cloth of his robe. He needed to leave or he'd be late, but his heart vibrated in sympathy for her.

He reached and broke the stem of a rose. Passing the flower to her fingers, he said, "Here. The rose is a symbol of God's grace. He will protect you in the—"

"He's never protected me before," she scoffed.

Shocked by her impious remark, Aidan floundered for a reply.

"But thank you anyway," she added. "You're kind. I'll . . . I'll smell it and let it remind me of the sun."

Aidan hurried to Vespers. It was a good thing he knew most of the hymns and prayers by heart, because his mind was not on them. He spent more of the worship musing about Lana than contemplating anything holy.

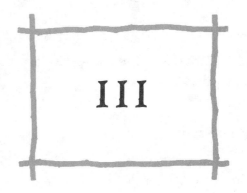

III

Rory caught Aidan's eye as Vespers ended and the monks were dismissed.

Novices were firmly discouraged from forming bonds with anyone except their confessor. Rory wasn't too much younger than Aidan, however, and he'd lived at the abbey as a servant before becoming a novice, so he overflowed with useful information. Aidan couldn't help being drawn to him. The pale boy had a quick wit and a secretive smile, although he buzzed so harshly of the number one that it set Aidan's teeth on edge. The fearsome noise didn't seem to match Rory's easy ways, so Aidan often wondered if his fellow novice was ill. Reluctant to explain his concern, he didn't dare ask. Rory's impish humor made up for the discomfort of being around him. The pair often swapped opinions about their chores, their meals, and certain of their brethren. Once in a while, they whispered together about a problem or confusion before drumming up the courage to discuss it with a more senior adviser.

Now, as the novices flowed out from their rear corner of the chapel, Rory lagged. He pretended to be transfixed by the carving of Saint Nevin on the lintel over the doorway. Aidan caught up with him. They both ducked out and jockeyed to walk side by side.

Because speech was strictly forbidden during meals, months ago they'd worked out a few subtle hand signs by which they could say hello, find out how the other was doing, and plan to meet for any hurried conversation that might not earn their masters' approval. They used these signals over short distances and in crowds as well as during meals, and now Aidan scratched his right ear, asking, "What is it?" as Rory trod alongside.

"You're looking reverent this evening, Brother Aidan," Rory murmured. This comment was also a code that meant the younger boy could see something weighing on Aidan's mind.

"Only troubled by the needs of the body," Aidan responded, without looking at him. Novices were taught to use those words when they needed to visit the privy.

Understanding, Rory trudged with Aidan and a few others toward the latrine. Both stepped back respectfully to let senior monks pass and then stood in single file as if awaiting a turn. Once the small double privy was empty, they could remain just outside it and talk. Going in would have meant that anyone approaching might have heard them, but once the first rush following prayers or a meal was over, the sight of not one but two people already in line was enough to turn others away, at least briefly.

"There's a girl here," Aidan murmured, without turning. "She's—"

Behind him, Rory choked. "In the privy?"

"No! In the abbey. Lord Donagh brought her, and it sounds as if she'll be staying."

When Rory didn't answer immediately, Aidan twisted his head to see why. At last the younger boy teased, "Careful, brother. Chastity in flesh and in thought."

Aidan groaned. "I'm sorry we ever talked about that."

Perhaps because he was younger or simply more self-controlled, Rory seemed amused by Aidan's struggle with the temptations of women. Those temptations so far had been only imagined, but that did not lessen their pull. Aidan had expected the lusty thoughts and dreams to fade once he'd committed himself solely to the company of other fellows, not counting the abbot's fat wife or Father Niall's crabby one. The reverse, if anything, seemed to be true. The more time passed, the more female shapes rose unbidden in his mind. He'd confessed it more than once and tried to follow Brother Eamon's advice. There were times, however, when the contemplation of God somehow turned into the contemplation of girls he had known. Aidan would hardly notice the shift until something, sometimes his own treacherous body, abruptly alerted him that he'd strayed.

Brother Eamon had kindly assured him that a firm will and the love of God would help him prevail. Rory, too, seemed bent on reminding him often and heartily, but Aidan wasn't so sure. At times only the complete lack of privacy stood between him and the kind of touching that his mentor called self-abuse. Since even the latrine had two seats, however, the temptation was quashed, if not by Aidan's will, then by others' watchful eyes.

"I just thought it was interesting," Aidan grumbled, trying to pretend there was no truth in Rory's assumption. "Girls don't arrive here every day. Forgive me for noticing."

"I forgive you, not that it will do you much good," Rory said amiably. " 'Tis not my forgiveness you need. But if I were God Almighty, I'd make the rules easier for you."

"Shh! Careful, yourself," Aidan said, glancing sharply toward the workshops behind them. Wool spinners and weavers were returning to conclude their day's labors but paying no attention to anyone near the latrine. "That's almost blasphemy to say you could do better than God."

"I think it *is* blasphemy, or it would be if I meant it." Rory's voice dropped. "But anyone can see that some of the rules come from men, not from God. How long would people inhabit His earth to worship Him if we were all pure and chaste? He'd have to create new men from mud."

Aidan chomped hard on a grin. "You think He'd rather put up with a few carnal sinners?"

"It was His idea, obviously. If we weren't meant to come together like animals, He could have made us more like plants." Rory brushed his toes through the dust, musing. "God is probably relieved when monks and priests just take wives and don't try to pretend. Fewer virgin births for the angels to herald that way."

"Ai. You'd better never talk like that around anyone else," Aidan warned, again eyeing the yard behind them. "Even the other novices might turn you in."

"Ah, that's why you'll take vows before I ever will, my brother. You're not more devoted. Just more cautious, I guess." He stepped past Aidan toward one side of the latrine.

Aidan stopped him with a grip on his arm. Rory's glib tone had fallen flat. The older novice looked for a jest in his friend's pallid gray eyes. None lay there.

"Do you question your calling, Rory?"

Rory gazed back, clearly wondering not how to answer, but whether he should.

"You can trust me," Aidan murmured. "I won't say anything."

With one hand, Rory smoothed the coarse cloth over

his chest. "I didn't have much choice about coming here," he said, speaking to the ground at their feet. "Less than you, even. My parents gave me and my younger brother to God so the rest wouldn't starve. But, Aidan—" He looked up. "Have you ever heard God's voice? Actually heard it speaking, I mean? Or an angel's?"

Aidan hesitated. The humming of numbers was not quite a voice, and although he hoped it came from God, he certainly didn't hear it as words.

"Not exactly," he said. He held his breath, gathering nerve to say more. "But I—"

"I have," Rory said, his face more unreadable than Aidan had ever seen it. "Once. I was told that I will face Christ's judgment in heaven before long and reminded to complete as much of His work as I can in the days I have left. That's why I always volunteer to hand out the alms to the hungry. But I doubt I will ever take the tonsure and have a bald place shaved on my head."

Aidan wanted to tell Rory he must have been wrong about the voice or its message. He couldn't do it. Even if he had never heard anything mystic himself, he had his own suspicions about his friend's health. Rory's admission confirmed them.

While Aidan gnawed his lip and wondered what else he could say, Rory grinned.

"That doesn't mean I want to see you go astray. If I'm

wrong, I'll just be a lay brother working the fields or cutting stone for the new church. Only tonsured monks get to be scribes. So I figure my good works should include keeping a sharp eye on your soul. Forget about that girl."

Rory pulled free and slipped inside the privy before Aidan could collect his wits to respond. His eyes scoured the packed earth of the yard while his mind retraced Rory's words. The idea that he was being watched and guided by a younger friend felt backward and shameful. Worse, he feared Rory was probably right.

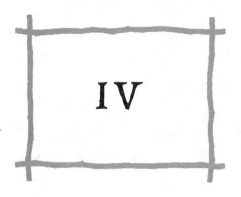

IV

Rory's shocking admission briefly pushed Lana from Aidan's mind. Not long after the two novices signaled a farewell outside the privy, however, she tripped back into his thoughts. Chores left him no time to wander before darkness and the first nighttime prayers. Afterward, on his way back to the hut that served as the novices' dormitory, Aidan took a detour. He hung back from those traipsing toward their beds and slipped away to the rose garden. It was indeed a dark night, but as he crept from one building or stone cell to the next, he unconsciously let his ears guide him. Not only the hidden monks but the wooden timbers, the grass thatch, and the roses hummed a muted trail of numbers to follow.

The brothers remained silent throughout the night, except for the Nocturns worship at midnight and Matins a few hours later, so he wouldn't be able to speak to her this time. But the memory of her fear and her fingers straining out of her cell, as though from an unfinished tomb, had haunted his prayer time. He wanted to check whether she had fallen asleep as advised.

She hadn't. As he made his way between the shadowy rosebushes, he heard her softly crooning an old song to herself. The notes drifted to him like the fabled music of faeries. Chills ran along his skin.

Perhaps he gasped or she heard his footsteps. The song stopped. Aidan had never before minded the strict silence that followed the last prayers of the day. Now words clogged in his throat. He wanted to ask her to continue her song. He'd heard plenty of monks singing in chapel, some with more talent than others, but he'd never heard a trilling like this. Her voice, harmonizing with the chimes of eleven, could have been that of an angel.

Struggling to keep his tongue still, he snapped another rose off its stem and passed it into the gap in the wall. Her hand was not there. Unsure if she'd notice his gift in the dark, he tapped his nails on the stone. This noise stretched the bounds of obedience, but he couldn't see how a little rapping of fingers differed so much from soft footfalls or the creak of a door.

She heard him. "Aidan?"

He couldn't reply, but he might not have answered anyway. He wanted to hear his name again in her silvery tones.

She didn't repeat herself. She did not sing again, either, though he waited so long he feared his absence from the dormitory might be noticed. He could feel her eleven-ness and her strangeness and her girlish defiance just on the other side of the thick stone wall. No rustling or even the sound of her breathing, however, escaped through the slot. He put his hand to it, but the stone was hard and rough and empty of both roses and fingers, other than his. So he pulled away and crept out of the garden, hoping she did not hear him leave.

The nighttime and predawn worship passed in a sleepy blur, as those hours often did. When Aidan awoke again in the morning, he forgot briefly that the abbey held anything different. Eagerness spiked through him as memory returned. He rose in haste and then slowed, telling himself he might as well forget again. He would likely never get closer to Lana or speak to her any more freely than he already had. Yesterday's risks had been disobedient and foolish. It occurred to him, belatedly, that her intriguing eleven-ness might even be the work of Satan, designed to tempt him from his duties, not to mention from the path that would lead him to the scriptorium someday.

His guilt took flight right after breakfast, when old Brother Nathan caught him on the way out of the Great Hall where they ate.

"See me after daily instructions," the stern monk told him.

Aidan nodded, struggling to keep his face from cramping in worry. A delayed punishment might be coming, and perhaps not just for hiding under a bench. Someone may have spotted him whispering with Lana yesterday.

Standing among the gathered monks, Aidan thought instructions would never end. The abbot rambled on about the state of the crops, preparations for winter, and next week's assignments for scrubbing the latrine. Aidan tried not to fidget and shuffle his feet. Distracted, he almost didn't notice the mention of his own name. The awareness of others' eyes on him honed his attention.

"Brother Aidan has been with us almost a year now," the abbot was saying. "His time as a novice is nearly done. Now his devotion and faith should be tested more severely. I want to make you all aware of a task set for him, that you might watch him and guide him if his feet seem even slightly to stray."

Aidan gulped, completely unprepared for anything Abbot Bartley might say. He knew that a novice's final weeks were a time of close scrutiny. He'd be questioned hard before he took his lifelong vows. Only satisfactory answers would permit him to have the peak of his skull shaved in the tonsure that marked a full-fledged monk. But he hadn't realized any other sort of test might be involved.

The abbot cast a glance at Brother Eamon, who simply nodded approval.

"A guest arrived here yesterday, one who may stay for a time," the abbot continued, frowning ever so slightly. Aidan closed his eyes to receive what was almost certainly coming: humiliation for lurking beneath a bench upon the visitor's arrival, then the assignment of penance disguised as a test.

As the abbot went on, not at all as Aidan expected, it took a minute for his ears to recover and listen.

"I remind you to remember your vows and treat this guest as though Christ Himself, in hooded robes, had come calling," the abbot said.

Aidan barely contained a nervous snicker. He'd heard guests described the same way before, but he'd never known any to be locked in the penitent's cell. He wondered if Jesus would have minded.

"To save you from being startled," Abbot Bartley continued, "I will make you aware that this guest is a particular young girl who will serve God and this abbey as a scullion in the kitchen."

The monks were far too disciplined to murmur, but a few scowls and raised eyebrows revealed their surprise.

"Most of you need not concern yourselves, nor should you speak with her, of course. As is our custom, one novice will take special charge of the guest's guidance and protection." The abbot's blithe tone grew firmer. "That duty befalls Brother Aidan."

Aware that his jaw had gaped but unable to close it, Aidan met the abbot's eyes. Abbot Bartley gazed back with serenity and a glint of mischief.

"Through this challenge, I think the strength of his calling and faith will be made clear."

The abbot made a few final announcements while Aidan's head swam. He could feel Rory poking a finger into the small of his back, somewhere far away, but the warning wasn't needed. The truth of what had seemed for an instant like a reward settled over him. Lana was troublesome—that was why she was here, even if he wasn't supposed to know that. It would be easy enough to show her the few places she would be permitted to go. But who could guess what new trouble she might cause? All of it would fall on his shoulders, and it would take only a slight lapse in attention or judgment for him to be barred not only from the scriptorium but perhaps from the monastery itself. Aidan's entire life had just been placed in the hands of an irreverent girl who'd already committed a crime, who didn't mind what she said about God to a monk, and who hummed of the number eleven.

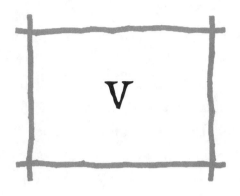

V

The abbot unbolted the door to the penitent cell, pulled it open to enter, and nearly tripped over Lana. Instead of lying on the dirt floor, she'd slept curled against the threshold.

"What are you doing down there, girl?" he asked. "Peeping out through a knothole?"

She got to her feet, drawing her wool mantle closer around her. Her eyes darted to Aidan and away as if afraid to rest there too long.

"The door is oak wood," she explained. "It was protecting me in the night."

Her odd answer caused the abbot to raise his eyebrows and press his lips tight. Wondering if the fat fellow understood her remark better than he did, Aidan barely listened while Bartley questioned her to determine if the sass and fire she'd displayed yesterday had been quelled. The novice was too busy scanning the dimly lit cell. The roses he'd passed her were nowhere in sight. He exhaled in secret relief. If the abbot had seen them, he would have demanded to know how she'd gotten them.

Aidan studied her from the corner of his eye. Lana's sleeveless shift had been made from a fine linen with intricately embroidered borders. A much poorer mantle of dusty lavender warmed her arms and guarded the honey-colored garment beneath. Both draped loosely over a frame that looked ill-fed, considering the quality of her shift. She'd tied her gingery hair back with a bit of red yarn. Another length of yarn circled her throat, dangling a small cross made of two twigs tied together. She held her neck straight and proud as though her necklace were a jewel, not stray bits of wood. Perhaps because of her parentage, she was an odd combination of urchin and beauty. Aidan was sharply aware of his own rough-spun robe, which he wore day and night as all the monks did. Tomorrow was wash day, so almost a week's dirt and sweat marked him today.

In all likelihood, she didn't notice, at least not right away. She kept her eyes low, with her hands clasped before her, and she answered the abbot humbly, assuring him that her hard night and a day without water or food had made her ready to follow a more righteous path. Only after Bartley had turned to Aidan did she peek up through her lashes to coolly gauge the effect of her words.

"Show her where to empty her chamber pot, Brother Aidan," said the abbot. "Then lead her to the High Cross where the people worship on Sunday, and finally to the kitchen. Those are the only places she should need to visit, except for the guesthouse, where you can convey her later tonight. Instruct her in the rules that apply to our guests. Brother Galen, in the kitchen, is prepared to set her to work."

A question struck Aidan so hard he flinched. He cast his eyes to the ground and licked his lips, afraid to ask his question and more afraid of the answer.

"What is it?" the abbot asked, seeing the hesitation. Aidan could feel Lana's curious gaze fall on him as well.

He murmured, "Shall I wash her feet first?" It was a customary service to guests upon their arrival. He'd done it many times, but the visiting feet had always been male. The idea of touching her skin sent a flush racing over his own.

"That will not be necessary in this case," the abbot said dryly.

Not sure if disappointment or relief drove the quick shiver down his back, Aidan dipped his head.

"You should see her briefly in the guesthouse each morning and evening to escort her en route to the kitchen. You may also answer her questions as needed—I repeat, briefly. I do not expect this to take much time from your usual duties. Bring any difficulties to me."

Aidan nodded, full of other questions he didn't dare

ask, afraid they would sound too much like protests. If the answers did not become clear, perhaps he'd get another chance to ask later.

The abbot turned sternly back to Lana. "When you are not in the kitchen with Brother Galen, Brother Aidan will help you as much as he can, but please remember that he has important work otherwise." The abbot eyed her, perhaps not completely convinced by the meek attitude she showed today. "Let me warn you: If you do not get along here like a mouse in a stable, unnoticed and harmless, he will suffer as much as you. Perhaps more."

"Suffer how?" she asked, taken aback.

"Brother Aidan can tell you anything else you need to know." After a polite but final tip of his head toward her, the abbot gave Aidan a cautionary look and trundled away.

"What did he mean?" Lana wanted to know. "Were you punished for talking to me yesterday?"

"Hush!" Aidan warned, peering over his shoulder at the abbot, who still might have been within earshot. He waved her back into the dim cell.

"I'm not sure anyone knows about that," Aidan admitted. "They have assigned you to me as a test."

"What are they testing?" she asked. "If I can get you in trouble or not?" Grinning, she reached up and ran her hand flirtatiously around his neck.

" 'Tis not funny," he said, jerking away from the tickle

her fingers left on his skin. "If you cause any problem, they'll blame me. They'll say my faith or devotion or prayers are weak, and I won't be allowed to take vows. I might even have to leave. Without anywhere to go, really." He didn't bother to mention the books he'd never be able to create.

"That's not very fair," she said.

He gave her a long stare he hoped would impress her with the difficulty of his position. "Just follow the rules. 'Tis not that hard."

"Well, I'm glad I got you and not some crusty old monk with no teeth," she declared. "So what are these rules anyway?"

"Get your chamber pot," he said. "I'll tell you on the way."

As she retrieved it, his eyes fell on the oaken door.

"What did you mean about sleeping next to the door?" he wondered.

She stroked one palm over the heavy, age-darkened wood.

"It still remembers the forest," she murmured. "It helped me remember, too—sunlight spilling through branches, acorns dropping, leaves dancing on the breeze. And 'tis warm. Everything else in this dreadful pile of stones is so cold." Her eyes jumped to his, guilt dancing briefly on her face. "Except your roses, of course," she added. "And you. I was grateful to have them yestereve."

Aidan shrugged, more interested in what she had said about the door. The heavy-grained wood made him think of winter and the supper table and the number twenty-six, not summer sunlight.

She saw his bemused look.

"You can't feel it, can you?" she asked. "If it is not the crucifix or the Ark, your people don't seem to care about wood. Just sins and confessions and tithes."

"My people?" he asked, startled by the disdain in her voice. "I'm the same as you." He did not add what surely they both knew: Under the circumstances, her father's nobility did not matter at all.

"Priests and monks, I mean."

Amazed and dismayed by her disapproval, he glanced outside for observers and whispered, "I'm not really here because I wanted to be a monk. I'm here to be a scribe."

"What's the difference?"

Suddenly annoyed by her barely concealed contempt, he showed her some of his own. "You wouldn't understand."

"Just as you don't understand the oak," she retorted. "Are you going to show me where to empty this, or shall I toss it on you?" She lifted the chamber pot toward him.

He backed away quickly. She laughed. He spun to leave, not caring if she followed or not.

"Don't be angry," she said, scurrying behind. "I was only teasing."

When he didn't relent, she added, "You know how to read, then? And write? I wish I could. I saw a book once."

"Just once?" Aidan sneered, trying without much success to mimic her earlier disdain. It didn't come naturally to him, and the ugly sound of it reminded him how ungodly he was being.

"You've seen many, I guess," she said. "I haven't. Only the one. I'll never forget. 'Twas beautiful, like wondrous stitching without thread."

The complete absence of contempt from her voice confused him. She switched from angry to earnest too quickly for him to keep up. He slowed, belatedly remembering that a monk should not show undue haste.

"My fa—I mean, Lord Donagh showed me," she added, falling in alongside him. "When I was a little girl. Sometimes he was kind to me then."

When she wasn't sharpening her tongue on him, Aidan wanted to cup her in his hands like a lost bird. He shoved that feeling aside, sure it couldn't be trusted.

"He showed you a kindness by bringing you here instead of fettering you in the stocks," he said quietly. He did not look over, though he could feel her eyes on him.

"You know about that?"

Aidan lifted one shoulder and dropped it.

"He did not do it for kindness. He doesn't want me soiling his honor."

"You're hardly his only bastard."

"I wish you wouldn't call me that," she murmured, then added, more firmly, "I'm the only one caught swindling pilgrims. And my mother and uncle won't let him give me away as a concubine, thankfully, so any value I might have had to him has been lost. I'm an embarrassment on both counts. But he cannot seem to resist my mother's favors. Nor she his."

Aidan ignored the bitterness in her voice. It sprang from hazardous topics he would prefer to avoid, since they might be overheard. Instead of replying directly, he waved her around a corner and said, "Splinters of the Cross, was it not? Why did you do that?"

"Because I thought I could," she said, casting him a world-wise glance. "The pilgrims have silver, and they're not shy of parting with it. How else are we supposed to come by our bread? My uncle spent his youth as a slave; he can barely provide for himself. And his lordship brings gifts for my mother now and again, but there are plenty of days in between."

That, Aidan thought, might explain the costly fabric covering her thin body. Her mother must have struggled to feed herself and her daughter, since no man would dare to look twice at any mistress Lord Donagh saw regularly.

"A share of his wealth is due you," he said. "The judge will uphold that."

"When he dies," she retorted. "Or certainly not before I marry. Until then, are my mother and I supposed to eat stones? I'm not a thief. It seemed easier to cozen the pilgrims."

Aidan answered only with sympathetic silence. Her position didn't excuse her crime, but it did help explain it. And he had encountered enough silly pilgrims at the abbey to understand her disdain. Some would sin with one hand and, with the other, pay for prayers or the right to touch relics they thought would absolve them.

"I want my wood fragments back," she added firmly. "Your abbot still has them, I guess. Can you get them for me?"

"I doubt it. What difference does it make?"

She eyed him, an answer almost visible on her lips. Apparently deciding she couldn't trust him that far, she set her jaw.

"I just want them. They may not come from the Holy Land, but they're special to me."

Intrigued, Aidan didn't consider his words carefully enough. "You shouldn't have been selling them, then." He regretted the comment even before she threw him a narrow-eyed glare.

"I will ask," he added, shrugging. "Don't be surprised if the answer is no."

He held his breath while she dumped her pot into the

stinking cesspool. They moved as quickly as they could back across the compound to replace her chamber pot. Aidan found it easier to speak to her once they'd again reached the shelter and shadows of buildings.

"Would you like to see another book?" he asked, after a moment.

The eager light in her eyes gave him a rush of warmth he couldn't admit, even to himself. He was sure it must be sinful.

He knew better than to try to take her to the scriptorium; even he was not allowed to interrupt the scribes' devotions. But he'd been instructed to show her the High Cross, after all, where the abbey's neighbors and pilgrims met to celebrate Mass. On the way, they could pass by the chapel.

The stone building was empty, as Aidan had hoped. Worship eight times a day left even the most devout with little will to visit between the Divine Hours, unless to do penance. One wizened monk guarded the relics most of the time, of course, but Aidan knew that he often made a leisurely visit to the privy about now. The shuffling fellow had returned several times to find Aidan admiring books, and he'd only shooed the novice away with a toothless smile. Aidan hoped his patience, if needed at all, would stretch a bit farther.

At the chapel's doorway, Aidan shushed Lana and

warned her not to set even a toe inside. Then he slipped alone to the altar, where he knelt, crossed himself, and whispered a heartfelt prayer before rising again. A Gospels lay on the altar before him. The nearby lectern held a Book of Hours and a missal as well. None were the abbey's finest, by any means; those were too valuable for daily use. But Aidan had inspected these volumes before, and even the worst earned his respect.

He brought the Book of Hours back to the doorway. After reminding her not to touch it, Aidan held the book for Lana to see and turned a few pages to show the illumination on several. He kept his ears tuned for footsteps.

"I can't believe you can read this," she breathed. "Or write it." She graced him with a look of open admiration.

"Well . . . most of it," he said, sinful pride tugging at him and tingling his scalp. It had not been easy to learn a language so different from what he spoke every day, and even more mind-boggling to capture spoken words from out of the air and shape them in ink. Making sounds into pictures that a reader could turn back into sounds felt to him almost like magic. Caressing a line of script with his thumb, he added, "I'm still learning."

When he glanced back up at her, she was studying him, not the illumination.

The book felt suddenly heavy and dangerous in his hands. He hurried to replace it. Once it rested on the lectern again, his heart pounded at the liberty he'd taken. He walked slowly back outside, pondering the loss of sense that Lana seemed to effect on him.

"And that's what you do all day?" she asked, when he drew close. "Draw words and cunning little patterns and creatures?"

"Not yet," he admitted. "But I will, once I've apprenticed enough. If you will help me by minding the rules," he added pointedly.

"You haven't told me any yet," she protested.

Forced to admit she was right, he finished her tour and then led her toward the kitchen, off by itself near the back gate because of the danger of fire. On the way he described the constraints of humility and modesty and the importance of washing and the many times to be quiet.

"Is there a tree drawn in one of those books?" she interrupted. "The Trees of Life or of Knowledge that Father Niall talks about?"

"Did you hear anything I've said?" he demanded.

A grin played on her face. "Some of it. I'll listen better after you answer my question."

Huffing, Aidan resisted the desire to stomp. Talking with her was nothing like talking to the other monks or novices, not even Rory. It reminded him more of horseplay with his brothers and sharp-tongued little sister at home.

How accustomed he'd grown to silence and nodding! A pang of homesickness amplified his annoyance.

He sulked until he realized that treating Lana to silence would only likely hurt him. Then he grumbled, "I don't remember any drawings of trees."

"Are you sure?" She reached a hand to his arm.

Aidan didn't know any books but the Psalter by heart, and some had illumination so complex the pages could be studied for hours and still reveal surprises. Plus there were plenty of volumes in the scriptorium he'd never touched.

"No," he said. "I'm not sure at all. There could be. Why?"

A crafty light crossed her face, but she shook her head. "I just wondered. Thank you for showing me. Now you'd better tell me your rules again. I don't want you to get into trouble over me. I'm used to it, but you're not. I can tell."

Feeling somehow insulted, though sure she hadn't meant it, Aidan replied, "Brother Galen is probably wondering where we are. Just do exactly what he says and stay in the kitchen or the yard right outside it. I'll come get you before the Hour of Compline tonight and tell you the rest—again—then."

She ignored his emphasis. "Will he give me something to eat, do you think?"

"Ask him," Aidan said, wincing at the pinched hope in

her face. "I'm sure he will. But don't speak to anyone else unless they speak to you first. Please."

"Just you?"

"Yes." A few steps later, he added, "And I speak to you too much. I've got to stop."

They hurried the rest of the way to the kitchen in silence.

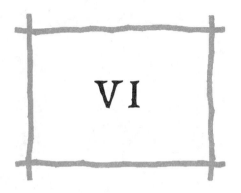

VI

"You neglected to see me after instructions," said Brother Nathan. He need not have bothered. Aidan had realized his error the moment the hawkish monk had hailed him from outside the scriptorium. He had been hurrying toward it after leaving Lana to her taskmaster, hoping he wasn't too late for a calligraphy lesson that morning. The chance to practice on a waxed wooden tablet was often the best part of his day.

At Nathan's call, Aidan had cringed, the memory of the monk's earlier request flooding back. He'd approached the scriptorium's master with his feet dragging. Brother Nathan's precise and unforgiving nine had whined at him the whole way.

"I forgot," Aidan groaned, dropping his gaze to the senior monk's hem and feeling his heart sink even lower. "Can you forgive my stupidity? I was so surprised by the abbot's instructions, I did not remember your request."

Aidan wondered if Brother Nathan, who knew Aidan had witnessed Lana's arrival, had played any role in that surprise.

If so, the older monk did not let a trace of amusement or understanding cross his face. "Your assignment," he said. "Yes. Well, I had an errand for you. But perhaps you've been burdened enough."

"Something for the scriptorium?" Aidan asked, unable to keep his eyes down or his voice from leaping in hope. It was exhilarating to know that Brother Nathan had even thought of him. Until now only a few younger scribes had deigned to encourage his interest. Aidan added, "I would still serve you, if I may."

Brother Nathan regarded him coolly. Aidan pressed his lips together and looked down again, resenting his own impulse to grovel.

"You no longer have time before our next prayers."

Hoping it would not sound like argument, Aidan ventured, "Is it something I might do following supper instead?" The hour after the midday meal was the monks' only free time, a rare chance to nap, enjoy a game of quoits, or listen to someone playing a pipe. He might regret giving it up.

By the time Nathan spoke again, Aidan was expecting a reprimand. His ears took an instant to confirm what sounded like a question.

"Perhaps. You roamed near here as a boy, did you not?"

Aidan nodded warily. He'd driven his father's cattle to summer pastures, played along the banks of the river, and hunted in the woods with his brothers and friends. Those days seemed a long time ago now.

"I thought so. Well, the scribes are running low on dark ink. Go gather oak apples, dry ones if possible, and you may learn how it is made."

Aidan turned bright eyes to the senior monk's face. "Truly?"

"A few dozen should do. Can you find them nearby and be back before the next worship this afternoon?"

Aidan's mind raced, trying to think where the nearest oak grove lay. "I think so."

"See that you do."

"I will. Thank you, Brother Nathan."

Nathan turned away. Aidan held his breath, afraid the older monk would change his mind. As if hearing that fear, Brother Nathan paused.

"This is the first time you've left here since becoming a novice, is it not?" he asked.

"Except for the fields," Aidan replied. Lord Donagh's forebears had granted the abbey a large tract of land, but tending crops or livestock alongside other monks was not the same as crossing common ground where he might meet old neighbors or kin.

Nathan pursed his lips. "Be alert, then, for distractions unbecoming a monk. I'd rather you returned empty-handed than with a confession."

Aidan agreed quickly. Compared to supervising Lana, he didn't expect this errand to prove much of a test. He waited until Nathan retreated, then sped to dispatch his daily chores so they couldn't delay him later. He kept his legs to a walk only with effort.

When Rory heard, in quick snatches on the way to their next prayers, that Aidan would be going out, his reaction took Aidan by surprise.

"Don't go," he murmured, jostling Aidan to get close enough so those around them wouldn't hear. Since Rory barely moved his lips, it took Aidan an instant to translate, "Tell Bro' Na'an you're ill. S'rain your ankle. Anything."

Aidan scratched his upper lip and said behind his hand, "No. I want to do his bidding. Why not?"

They turned a corner, out from under the watch of Brother Eamon a few paces behind them. "I have never been outside since I've been a novice, nor has any I know," Rory said. "He could send a servant instead. They may not be merely testing you, Aidan. They might be setting you up."

Aidan stole a sidelong glance, trying to interpret Rory's scowl. "You're just jealous."

Rory nodded vigorously. "Yes, that too. But I have a bad feeling today, and mostly I'm worried you will err so seriously that I'll be alone here again. That would be a foul disappointment."

"Thanks for the confid—"

By then, however, their fellows behind them had turned the corner as well.

"Brother Rory," called Brother Eamon, "are you having difficulty walking that you must crowd those around you?"

With a wince, Rory stopped and turned while Aidan kept walking.

"I'm sorry," he replied. "I was just telling Brother Aidan how much I value his example as he is tested prior to vows."

Aidan mashed a grin, glad his mentor walked at his back and thus couldn't see it. His friend was quite practiced at explaining a lapse in obedience without actually telling a lie.

"I see," Brother Eamon said dryly. "But perhaps you should speak less and follow that example with a little more space between you."

After that, Rory and Aidan kept their distance, not daring to attract attention twice in the same day. The hours and prayers before supper dragged. During the meal, Aidan had to count silently to ten in Latin between every bite of his boiled bacon and cabbage to prevent himself from wolfing the food. The voice of the scripture reader droned in the background. Rory darted concerned glances down the table toward Aidan, rubbing one eye and then the other. Aidan took this confused gesture to mean that he should watch out, but his friend's agitation was almost insulting. The senior monks were giving Aidan chances to fail, perhaps, but also to prove himself. If he could satisfy Brother Nathan, the scriptorium would move that much nearer his reach. He resolved to show only devotion. As long as he did what he was told, and stopped thinking of Lana as anything but a burden to bear, he'd be fine.

When the monks were dismissed from supper, he tried to send Rory a reassuring smile. He completely ignored the signals his friend sent in return, a request to meet at the privy. Instead Aidan headed directly for the abbey's back gate, which stood nearer the woods. He was worried about running out of time and returning either empty-handed or late.

Emerging through the high embankment that circled the compound, Aidan felt curiously naked. Even the autumn sun seemed to recognize a monk out of place. It peeped at him from behind one cloud, came out to stare directly, then ducked away behind another.

He walked tentatively past a few huts and noisy crafts-men's sheds, soon passing into the fields. Then Aidan jerked up the hem of his robe and ran. He needed to go fast to be sure he got back on time, but more than that he needed to feel his muscles doing work other than plowing and weeding and scraping calfskin. He sprinted until his lungs hurt and sweat tickled him under his robe.

He'd dropped back to a walk before it occurred to him that he hadn't been gone for ten minutes and he'd already succumbed to a distraction unbecoming a monk. For Aidan, the monks' insistence on thoughtful, unhurried movement was harder to abide than unquestioning obedience or silent meals or nearly anything else. He told himself speed had been necessary, not frivolous, if he was to obey Brother Nathan and be back before the next worship.

Bent figures cut and bundled oats in the distance. The harvesting monks took no notice of Aidan as he ducked into the woods, relieved not to have met anyone else. The smell of sun-warmed bark and molding leaves enveloped him. Good memories welled up inside him in response. As a boy he'd spent long afternoons playing in the woods with his brother Gabriel, climbing trees and pretending to be warriors. Now Aidan was struck by how much he missed not only his family but the hillsides and vales and creeks. The flickering forest was a welcome change from the constraints of the abbey. He wandered amid the crackling autumn leaves, a smile on his face belying the pinch in his heart.

He soon found a cluster of oaks, not as far from the abbey as he'd feared. The oak apples were plentiful on the ground or still clinging to branches within reach, and the small wasp that had grown within each had left long ago. Pulling up a fold of his robe, Aidan dropped the green and brown lumps into the makeshift pouch. He enjoyed picking out their number, twenty-seven, which whispered to him amid the chorus of birdsong and wind's sigh and other numbers, most in the twenties and thirties, that swirled through the forest.

When Aidan could no longer add oak apples to his cache without the same quantity spilling back out, he straightened and adjusted the load against his belly, wondering if he had enough.

"I hope you're not planning to eat those."

Aidan whirled. Standing behind him, having watched for who knew how long, was Lana.

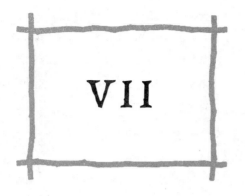

VII

Aidan stared. It took several long seconds for him to overcome his surprise enough to speak. He had been so focused on the sound of twenty-seven that he had not heard the whir of her eleven behind him. Certainly he heard it now, verifying the tale his eyes told.

"What are you doing here?"

Lana moved closer. "I saw you running. So I followed."

"You fol— You're supposed to be in the kitchen!" Rory's words came back to him, and his astonishment rolled into suspicion. He cast his gaze into the shadowy trees, looking for spies.

"Did they send you after me?" he wondered, dropping his voice. "Are you here to tempt me or something?"

Her eyebrows shot up, then a smirk rose on her lips. "This is Glendermor Wood, not the Garden of Eden. And you're the one with the fruit, though I don't think it—"

"Stop playing games. Why did you follow me?"

She huffed. "I was sent to the well. The back gate to the fields was unguarded, so I ran. I was already half escaped by the time I saw you."

He blinked, dubious. "So they don't know you're gone? Nobody sent you?"

"Well, they've probably noticed by now. There was shouting somewhere behind me."

Aidan groaned. That meant he'd be paying a price, maybe even getting the whip. "I'll probably be lashed over you!"

A fold appeared in her brow. "Aren't you running away, too?"

"Of course not! I was sent on an errand, that's all!"

"Oh." Disappointment lay clearly over her face—disappointment and sudden mistrust. She backed up a step. "Well, I'm sorry you'll be punished on my account. Truly I am. Will they really flog you? I thought monks were supposed to be kind."

He turned away with a frustrated snort. "They'll say my soul matters more than my skin." Sun dappled the trees all around them, and the dancing light made the clearing and Lana both seem unreal. Aidan prayed this might turn out to be a dream. But the thumping of his chest and the sound of his own breathing were too strong for any illusion.

"But you're not a prisoner," Lana added. "I am. And I hate it. So I'm running away, even if you're not."

"Donagh will just find you again."

"Not if I go far enough," she replied. "Not if I hide."

Concern uncoiled through the anger and amazement in his chest. "Where? And what will you eat? Where will you sleep?"

" 'Tis not winter yet. I know my way in the woods. There are hazelnuts and berries, wild carrots and garlic. And I can steal leeks and turnips by night."

Aidan regarded her, trying not to be impressed by her calm and almost sorry to feel his anger fading.

"The woods are full of rogues at night, Lana. Bandits and worse. You can't go about by yourself. You'll be hurt, if not killed."

Her face never shifted, but a tight swallow gave away her own fears. "I thought your God would protect me?" she asked. Her sarcasm failed.

Aidan didn't bother to answer. He dumped the oak apples and eased toward her, afraid she might bolt. Wary, Lana stood her ground. Aidan looked her square in the face and reached to take both her shoulders as if reasoning with an obstinate child. The wool of her mantle was unexpectedly thin under his fingers, betraying the tension beneath it. Her eyes latched onto his, and Aidan could feel her desperation pushing past her bold front.

"You can't," he repeated, more softly. "Just go back now to the abbey. You'll probably be punished, but not beaten or starved or left in a heap by men with no decency."

She studied his eyes. Aidan wished she wouldn't. Realizing how little space separated her body from his, he felt blood pounding through his neck and down every limb.

"Why do you care?" she whispered. Her breath smelled of the creamy cheese that Brother Galen must have fed her.

Several safe answers occurred to Aidan but could not find the way to his lips. At such close range, her high-pitched, trickish eleven seeped in through his ears and muddied his brain.

"You're an eleven." He heard the words as if someone else had spoken them. "I've never met an eleven before."

Her face puckered. "What's that supposed to mean?"

Feeling exposed and out of control, Aidan let go of her arms and turned abruptly to retrieve his oak apples. He was in danger of forgetting himself and his duties. What if he'd been right about spies, and some hidden monk watched from the trees?

"Never mind. Do what you will. I've got to get back." He shot her a glare. "If they'll still have me, once the abbot learns you've escaped."

She crouched to help him, infuriating him.

"Come with me instead," she said softly.

"Be serious."

"I am serious," she told him. She continued gingerly, as though stepping out on a wobbly bridge. "We'll be safer together. We could pretend to be pilgrims. The churches, at least, will feed us if we—"

"What makes you think I want to leave? I'm supposed to take my vows soon. I want to be a monk and work in the scriptorium!"

Lana lifted oak apples into the fold of his robe. Without looking at his face, she asked, "Then why haven't you spoken a single word of God or your love of Him to me?"

He stammered, sure she must be mistaken but unable to think of an example.

She added, gently, "We've talked more of my sinful father than your holy one."

"I'm a monk, not a priest," he growled, not understanding why her words were making him angry. "Not even that, yet."

Reaching into a pocket of her mantle, she drew out a handful of crimped rose petals. Through the haze of frustration in Aidan's head, the puddle of red yelped forty-four at him.

"I'd better give these back to you," she murmured. "You may need God's grace more than I do, Aidan."

Confused and defensive, he let his gaze bounce between the spill of color in her palm to her face. He almost hadn't heard her words. The red forty-four zinging at him from her palm resonated with the undernote of four in Lana's eleven, whisking his breath away. The harmony sang of blood and pain, but also of an irresistible fire in the cold universe.

"There's that look in your eyes again," she said. "What is it?"

"Nothing," he protested, appalled that she had spied his distraction.

"No, 'tis not nothing. You sometimes look at me as if it is all you can do not to—"

He grabbed her wrist, his hand flashing before he could stop it. The rose petals scattered, thankfully muting their hum.

"Not do what?" he hissed. "What I'd like to do right now is slap you. I know I would not be the first."

She nibbled her lips, looking not afraid but suddenly shy. Her knee pressed into the dirt. Before Aidan could react, she leaned forward to brush her lips against his flushed cheekbone.

"That," she said, not lifting her eyes from the ground.

Aidan couldn't breathe. One moment he itched to strike her, the next he wanted to wrap himself in her fair, eleven-ish skin, envisioning things worth a month of confessions. He jumped up the moment his legs would obey him, forgetting to keep hold of his robe. The oak apples spilled again. Lana cringed. Not finding some accusation he wanted, he spun on his heel, but his feet would not carry him farther. He closed his eyes, bowed his head, and folded his arms tight over his chest, fighting himself. He had to find some grace that would lead him through this completely unexpected trial. Where was the Holy Spirit when he needed a beacon?

"I'm making you unhappy. I'm sorry," came her voice, soft, from below. Movement rustled behind him. "I'll go."

Aidan prayed for help not to turn back around, but either the prayer or the Divinity failed him. She'd risen and fled a few paces away, walking backward to watch him. Her determined face lit when she saw him turn. That shine in her eyes drove a hot spike through Aidan's body as tangible as the thrust of a spear. He knew he was lost.

"Don't leave," he said.

"What else can I do?"

He raised his hands to his face, hiding it.

"Don't look at me. Just let me think."

He might as well have asked her to let him fly, but after a moment of blind silence, with only the sound of the wind laughing in the trees, thoughts shuddered back into his head. He held still and tried not to chase them, hoping they'd settle and then follow, one on the other, as they once had done routinely.

When he finally lowered his hands, he was startled to find her within arm's length again. "Don't stand so near me," he pleaded.

Her face twisted in dismay, but she took a few steps back.

"Listen to me," he said, keeping his eyes fixed on the ground at their feet. "Let me take you back to the abbey and tell them I caught you. That's the only thing that might save me. I spoke to you of the Gospels, and Christ moved your willful heart, and you saw your mistake. They won't punish you much if you can convince them you've become filled with the Spirit. I can give you words to say. All right?"

"That would be lying, Aidan." She sounded amused, sparking his fury again.

"Go tell the truth to the Devil, then. That's the best I can do." He snatched up the accursed oak apples once more. She didn't help this time, but she didn't leave, either. When he rose, his robe weighted, he was careful not to look at her. He spun and strode away as fast as he could.

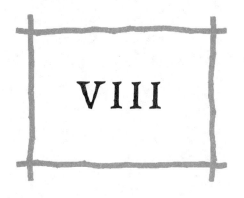

VIII

Aidan might have more easily escaped Lana if he'd had both hands free to cover his ears.

"I'll go back with you," she said, trailing behind him. "As you said. On one condition."

Disbelief bubbled into his throat, choking him. She had a lot of nerve, setting conditions. "What?"

"You teach me to read."

Laughter leapt from Aidan and he almost spilled the oak apples yet again. He threw his free arm over his face to hold in the immodest sounds. His sleeve muffled them well enough, but the trapped foolery ricocheted inside him, flattening his anger and the fear behind it.

"Why not?" she demanded. "Learned women are judges and poets and scholars, and I've even heard of churches led by women bishops and priests."

Aidan exhaled hard, struggling to control his voice.

Moving forward again, he said, "Go ask them to teach you to read, then. When will I have time or freedom to do it? If the abbot lets me back in at all, I'll probably be stuck in a penitent's cell for a week. You might be locked up for good. I won't dare say two words to you."

He risked a quick glance toward her. Stubbornness stamped her face.

"What do you want with reading, anyway?" he wondered.

"There's a part of your Bible I want to read for myself."

Aidan gaped, not sure she wasn't taunting. "Which part? Why?"

"Where it speaks about the Tree of Knowledge," she said.

Still doubtful, he replied, "Scripture is no matter for jest."

" 'Tis no jest," she said, hurrying to keep up with his long strides. "See, we call hazels the Tree of Wisdom, but I'm not sure that's the same. Do you think the words might have changed? Father Niall tells about the first woman biting an apple. But I've eaten apples. They don't make you any smarter that I noticed."

"It is not about being smart," Aidan told her. "The tree you mean was the Tree of Knowledge of Good and Evil— knowing right from wrong. That's why Adam and Eve had to cover their nakedness. They suddenly understood it was wrong."

She gave him a long look, and he thought for an instant she was going to argue with him. It would be just like her to declare nothing wrong with nakedness. Instead, she replied, "I think the real fruit might have been hazelnuts. There are many tales about hazelnuts bringing knowledge into the world. And divining, of course. You can divine almost anything with the right hazel rod: metal and water and jewels, or danger and thieves. . . ."

He grinned, amused by her simple folk beliefs. He'd watched the divining of water himself, but the rest were little more than charlatans' tricks. "Good things and evil ones?" he teased.

"Yes." Her eyes flashed at his gentle mocking. "You said something before, something strange," she went on. "You said I was eleven. Obviously I am not eleven years old. What did you mean by that?"

His grin fading, he watched the forest soil beneath his feet for several long strides. He didn't want to hand her a weapon she could use against him, and he feared he'd be doing just that if he told her the truth. Yet she had answered his questions honestly enough.

"If I tell you, will you come back to the abbey?" he asked, not trusting the evidence that she seemed to be following him there anyway. "And behave?"

"If you have any chance to teach me to read, any chance at all, will you do it?" she countered.

"Fine." He shrugged, never believing for a moment that it would come to pass.

"Good," she agreed. "We have a deal. So what's eleven? And then you can tell me what to say when we get there."

Aidan squinted, trying out words in his mind before voicing them. "Did you ever hear a sound," he began, "a harsh sound, maybe, that you could almost feel on your skin?"

"Like rocks scraping? Sure. Or hammering at the smithy."

"When I look at different people or things, I can hear a sound like that, a sort of buzzing around them. Hear it or feel it, or both. Different things make different sounds, and every sound is a number. Objects sometimes confuse me because they're quiet and they hum more than one sound at a time and I don't really understand how they add up. But people are loud, and their numbers are easy. My best friends have always been threes. My mother's a four. Your father's an eight. I don't trust people who make me hear seven. They're smart but they're—" He stopped, realizing he was beginning to babble. "I'm not explaining this very well."

"Well . . . maybe not," she said. "But I think I understand what you mean."

Her words hooked him like a fish. He breathed carefully, not wanting to disrupt the novel sensation that someone had even tried to understand.

She caught his eye. "So you hear eleven when you look at me?"

"Yes. High and sharp. I've been hearing numbers my whole life, and I've never met a person higher than ten."

"Eleven is a magic number, you know," she said, after a moment. "Powerful magic."

Aidan knew little of numerology beyond the numbers that repeated themselves in the Gospels, fours and sevens and twelves, but he believed her. He could hear the potency of her number in its sound.

"Thank you, Aidan," she added. "I think that's a compliment. It makes me—" She jerked to a stop, her head rising into the breeze.

"Do you smell that?"

Aidan inhaled. His nose caught the same seared air. A spike of alarm passed through him as his memory interpreted the scent.

"That's not wood smoke," he said. "That smells like fields burning!"

"Or thatch!" She ran a few paces, then whirled back toward him. "Oh, Aidan, not raiders . . . is it?"

His mind raced, trying to find another explanation, one that wouldn't carry so much dread. He noticed, then, the hush that had befallen the woods along with the smell of burning. Not a bird tweeped. He released his collected oak apples once more, hoping fervently he'd be picking them up again soon.

Seeing them spill, Lana tensed to bolt. He grabbed her.

She pulled him several steps before he managed to yank her to a halt, his lips near her ear.

"It might be," he said, low. He scanned the forest around them. "It might be Vikings, Lana, and if we're not careful we'll be dead."

She whimpered. "Or worse."

He let his eyes touch the pale skin of her throat. Instinct flared within him, leaving his muscles tingling and primed for a fight. He felt protective of her, even possessive. For the first time, his body's reaction to her did not make him feel guilty. "Yes. Come on." He pulled her into the shelter of the nearest tree.

"No. Not this one," she said, glancing up to its boughs. Pulling from his grip, she darted to another tree not far ahead.

Too worried to be annoyed, Aidan followed, searching for any hint that they weren't alone. Foreign raiders had never attacked within his memory, but he'd heard plenty of stories, horrific stories, from not far downriver. Fearsome and implacable pirates, the Norsemen swept down upon farm holdings and monasteries alike, marauding faster than local men could muster. They stole every item of value they could carry, torched anything that would burn, raped women, took slaves, and slaughtered anyone who got in the way. Aidan sent a quick prayer that if the river had conveyed such menace here, his family would stay far out of its reach.

"Don't run wild," he said, as much to himself as to Lana. "It might just be a cottage fire or something." He double-checked his bearings. "Stay here, out of sight. I'm going to the edge of the wood to take a look."

"No, don't leave me alone!"

His feet already in motion, he jittered to a stop and looked back. "Well, come on then!"

"Wait. I'm almost done." Lana had plucked a small branch from the tree and was busily snapping off twigs and stripping its bark with her teeth.

"Done with what?" He watched an instant without recognizing the Y-shaped bit of wood she'd formed. "Whatever it is, there's not time."

"You want to walk right into them?" she demanded. "Just be still a minute." Holding her hands over her head, she balanced one leg of the twig on the pad of each thumb and pointed its stem toward the sky. She pivoted in place, her eyes closed and her feet mincing in a small circle.

With a start, Aidan realized she had created a makeshift divining rod like those used to site wells. "You're dowsing water?" he demanded, uncomprehending. "Now?"

"Not water," she retorted. "Danger." The stem of the wand dropped abruptly to point almost due east. She opened her eyes to see where she and her divining rod faced. " 'Tis hazel wood, and it has never been wrong for me, Aidan. Whatever it is, it lies that way. And not very far!"

"The abbey lies that way," he said, a chill tickling his shoulders.

"Then we can't go there."

"Don't be stupid! If it is the Norsemen, the only place that might be safe is behind the abbey's ramparts."

"It is *not* safe, not now. Or else they're between it and here." She clutched Aidan's arm. "Do you think they might have already hit the homes just downriver?" Her voice careened higher, rasping of one. The jagged sound of that number made it hard for Aidan to think.

"It might be nothing," he said, although his instincts said different. "Listen. Let's . . ." He wanted to simply head back the direction he'd come, but her conviction was too powerful to ignore completely. "Let's circle around south, toward Kilcarrick Hill. From that vantage we can see what's on fire." He didn't add that from there it would be a relatively short, downhill dash to the abbey if need be.

Lana never released her clutch on his sleeve as they sprinted through the trees. Aidan drew her into the shadows of tree trunks and scouted a clear path to the next, then they ran and ducked again. The need to hurry and the desire to hide tugged equally at them. The stench of burning grew thicker by the moment.

Finally the land sloped up under their feet. Aidan could see blue sky beyond the last clump of trees on the shoulder of the stony hill. He'd just plotted the way in his mind when a bell sounded. Its peals were not the familiar, measured tones calling monks to their afternoon prayers. Instead the bell clanged in frenzied, toneless panic.

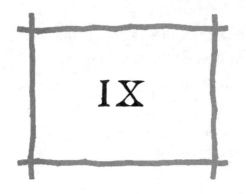

IX

Aidan stood frozen as the bell's clamor drifted to them on the breeze. A haze of smoke accompanied it.

"What does it mean?" Lana whispered.

"It means we're in trouble." Not even an abbey building ablaze would drive the monks to batter the bell like that.

"I could have told you that!" she hissed. "What are we going to do?"

Instead of answering, he brushed her grip off his arm and darted the rest of the way up the hill toward the clearing. He couldn't stand not knowing what was happening in the land below them.

Breaking from the cover of trees left him feeling abruptly exposed. He dropped to a crouch and scrabbled through the heather and rocks, reminded forcefully of playing Lambs and Wolves as a boy. Like real lambs, however, the losers of this game would bleed. Trying to keep his head down, he skirted the ridge at a slant until he could see past the hill's girdle of greenery. He tripped over the hem of his robe and skidded to his knees.

Aidan stared. In the distance, roiling smoke clouded what should have been a view of the river bend and the scattered homes and farmsteads beyond. Orange flames licked at the barley and oats not in one field, but many. Not a soul dotted the fields—if he didn't count a few dark, inexplicable heaps. Aidan tried to keep his eyes off those limp forms. He did not want to think what or who they might be. The abbey's earthen ramparts stood defiant, but he could see over the embankment to the buildings inside. Figures darted between walls and through doorways, hurtling in panic or rage but too distant to identify as either monks or intruders. Beyond, higher on the opposite hillside, Aidan could just make out the earthen defenses around Donagh's stronghold. The angle and distance hid any activity there, but Aidan didn't need to see it. Although the lord's ring fort may not have contained as much gold as the abbey, it represented control of the region. If the Norsemen hadn't clashed with Donagh's warriors and servants already, they soon would.

As Lana caught up to him, the abbey bell stopped. The sudden silence was even more unnerving than the wild clanging had been. With any warning, the monks should have gathered their valuables and barricaded whoever would fit in the souterrain excavated for exactly that purpose. If the bell had been ringing to summon those in the fields, anyone still outside was too late. Aidan fervently hoped that explained the bell's silence. The alternative was too grim to admit.

Either way, he and Lana were left on their own. He wouldn't dare cross the expanse of fields below, even at a dead run, without knowing for certain whether monks or raiders held the abbey. And towing Lana behind him would be like waving gizzards at vultures.

She took one look toward the tumbling smoke and burst into tears.

He hushed her quickly. "Just because we can't see them doesn't mean they aren't within earshot below us," he hissed.

"I'm sorry," she sobbed, muffling herself with her hand. "But the houses . . . my mother! How can we help them or know who's all right and who's not?"

"We can't." Aidan dropped his forehead into his hand. He prayed that his father and brothers had been working a field together, preferably with scythes and sickles at hand. Together they might have a chance of protecting themselves or their women and homes. Pressing that hopeful scenario into his heart, Aidan shoved aside the urge to know what really had happened. Unarmed, it would be suicide to go down into the smoke right now to find out.

"We can't," he repeated, trying to convince his twitchy legs. They wanted to run and know the worst. "Not yet."

"What do we do, then?" Lana choked back her tears.

"We've got to find somewhere to hide," he said, thinking aloud. "They might not move on right away. Or they may keep going upstream and return." He scoured the riverbanks for boats. He couldn't spot any through the smoke, but it would not have been hard to conceal them on the reedy and willow-draped banks.

"My father's house," she sniffed, wiping her dripping nose. "His guards will protect us. If he's not already d—"

Aidan spoke quickly before she released that word into the air. "We'd never cross the upper meadows without being seen. They'll get there long before we could—if they're not there already, laughing and drinking mead at his fire." He shook his head against the more likely scenes of pillage his mind had suggested.

"Oh! I know where we could go," Lana declared. "Follow me."

She scrambled back toward the cover of trees. Halfway, she cast a glance over her shoulder and stopped. She jerked her hand, not understanding why he hadn't followed.

Aidan hesitated, feeling the weight of the decisions before them. A wrong choice, an unlucky choice, might lead to an ax in the head. He jumped after her, not to follow but to confer. She didn't wait. The moment she saw him move, Lana was running again.

As he ran, crouched, to catch up, Aidan prayed for ideas. Lana was fleet, so they were dodging trees by the time he caught her and pulled her to a stop.

"Where are you going?" he demanded, trying to keep his voice low.

"I know somewhere safe in the woods below my father's house. Raiders would have no reason to go there, if they weren't actually following us, and they couldn't find it in any case."

"Where is it?"

" 'Tis secret. I'll show you."

"The beekeeper's cottage?"

"No. You're wasting time." She pulled from his hold and darted ahead. "You'll have to trust me. Come on."

Aidan didn't trust her at all, but he didn't have a better idea—at least, not until they had the cover of night. He did convince her to slow their pace for quiet's sake. She led him back down the hill and roundabout through the woods. When a bird flushed unexpectedly or the forest rustled too loud, they both froze. The first time, Lana's hand clutched Aidan's. Even once they moved on, he kept gripping her fingers. With that physical link between them, he could spend less effort following her and more sorting the light from the shadows. Afternoon sun mottled the branches and trunks all around them, and every movement hinted of danger.

Lana stopped twice to try her divining rod, which she'd carried the whole time. The first time, the result was roughly the same as before. The second time, though, the rod pointed almost directly ahead in their path. She blanched and dropped to a squat where she stood.

Aidan hunkered alongside her.

"They're close. I think they're coming this way," she breathed.

"Why do you say so?"

"I can feel it in the wood, through my hands," she replied. She crushed the rod to her chest and her eyes darted at the trees in their midst, looking for a way to escape. Aidan could see from her jerky trembling that she was approaching a panic. He put a hand on her shoulder.

"We're still all right," he assured her. "Backtrack? Go around?"

"No time," she whispered. Her eyes fixed on a large oak tree as though it were a raft that might save her from drowning. She jumped to it.

"Why don't we just hide for a moment and see if we hear anything?" He tried not to let impatience sharpen his voice, but he thought her imagination had slipped loose.

"No. We've got to climb," she insisted. When she turned her wide eyes back to him, a quake of apprehension ran through him. It was impossible not to catch some of her fear.

"All right." He followed her to the base of the tree.

"I don't know if I can reach the fork, though. Can you boost me?"

Aidan glanced around. "That one would be easier to climb."

"That one's not oak. Oak protects best. Will you help me or not?"

"Of course." He told himself they could simply rest in the tree until she had calmed. "Come on."

Lana braced her palms on the tree's ridged bark and tried to plant one sole against a bulge in the trunk. Her foot slipped off immediately.

"Here," Aidan said, forming a step with his interlocked hands. "Climb up from here."

She obeyed, and he lifted her as she shimmied upward until his hands were as high as his chest and she'd finally found purchase for all of her limbs. He tried not to see her curved calves flashing near his face. She climbed higher onto one of the heavy branches and turned to check the direction of danger, then peered back down at him.

"Can you get up here by yourself?" she whispered, her face stricken. "You must, Aidan!"

Aidan wasn't sure, but he vowed not to fail with her watching. Instead of trying to clamber directly into the high fork without much to grip, he jumped for the nearest branch and hung there briefly until he could swing his feet up as well. Silently cursing the length of his robe, he scrambled and pulled himself atop the branch. Satisfied, Lana climbed as high as she dared toward the top, where most of the tree's leaves still clung. Aidan followed, the skin along the insides and backs of his legs stinging where he'd scraped them on the bark.

"Don't fall," he warned. "This should be high enough." A patchy curtain of gold and brown leaves, belonging both to this tree and others, veiled the view in almost every direction. Bare spots on the branches opened windows toward the ground near the base of the tree and back the direction they'd come.

"No, it is not. Third fork or above." Checking his place, she added, "Come up where I can reach you." When he drew close enough, she plucked three oak leaves and passed them to him. "Put these under your robe, against your heart," she ordered.

His face wrinkled in doubt. "You jest."

"Do it!"

He watched her rip another three leaves and tuck them into the bodice of her shift.

"Hush now. Be still." She laid her cheek along the branch between her arms and closed her eyes.

A nervous smile popped to Aidan's lips. He didn't bother

to whisper that she'd be no less visible with eyes closed than with them open. The woods may indeed have hidden a threat, but they'd traveled far enough for Aidan to expect it from behind or alongside them, not from ahead.

Then he heard someone approaching.

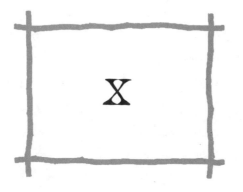

X

Aidan's smile vanished at the crackling coming toward them through the forest. His hand flashed to the neck of his robe and stuffed in the oak leaves as Lana had commanded. Then he held both the tree and his breath as tight as he could.

The first creature to burst into view below them was a hunting dog, limping and bleeding. It glanced up at them without interest as it shuffled past. A moment later, the unmistakable patter of human feet crunched below. Ice seemed to form in Aidan's veins, freezing hard and stiff so he couldn't move. Glad for his dingy gray robe in the branches and wishing Lana's purple mantle was also colored more like a tree, he watched in horrified silence as six or eight hulking men trotted below.

Aidan blocked all numbers from his ears and his mind. That blankness calmed a sudden, irrational fear that if he heard the humming of those passing below, they would somehow hear him in return. The raiders crossed at an angle to the direction Lana had been leading, presumably hurrying back toward the river from somewhere in the heights. The tree's leaves and branches revealed only glimpses: leather short-coats and helmets, a flash of bright breeches, thick snarls of dark hair. A bulging sack of some booty clunked against calves in tightly wrapped leggings. A blood-splattered battle-ax rested on a blood-splattered shoulder. Close behind it, one shrouded head declared a captive bound for slavery. Aidan stared, unable to shift his eyes, until the invaders had passed. Afraid his frozen muscles would fail and he'd slide out of the tree with a thump loud enough to turn them around, he pressed his forehead into the bark near his face. He could still hear the creaking of leather armor and the rattle of swords against brush.

The oak sheltered the pair, immobile, for long minutes until a ruffled squirrel chattered his irritation in the raiders' wake. Thawing at that familiar sound, Aidan looked over to Lana. She still had her eyes closed.

"I think we're okay," he whispered. "They must have come from Donagh's stronghold, above. Good thing we didn't try for that. You should have told me we'd have to cross between it and the abbey to get to your hiding place." In fact, he realized now, she had said something like that, but in his agitation he hadn't considered what it might mean.

She opened her eyes but only stared, her gaze far off and vacant.

"Lana?" he asked, worried.

"You didn't believe me," she said, after a moment. "I could see you dead in my mind because you wouldn't listen."

Aidan shivered. "I believe you now."

He'd passed too many long, silent seconds with only the sound of his pulse beating in his ears, echoing the tramping of feet. His mind had been working. Now he bit his lip.

"Are you a witch, Lana?"

She blinked at him, her dazed expression falling away. A closed caution replaced it.

"Father Niall says witchcraft does not exist," she told him. "He says it is a sin to believe that it does."

Aidan's eyes narrowed. She hadn't exactly answered his question. And despite what the Father might say, everyone Aidan knew believed that evil could find humans to work through. Maybe that explained her eleven hum. The moment that idea flashed in his mind, he had to dismiss it, again. Lana's radiant, singing eleven couldn't be evil.

"I'm not accusing you," he murmured. "You probably just saved our lives."

"Stop looking at me like that, then."

"I just wondered where you learned that trick with the

hazel rod. I thought divining was only for water." When she didn't answer, he added, "Lana? Tell me. Are you?"

She pressed her lips tight, set her jaw, and started climbing down from the tree.

"I've never seen the Devil and I wouldn't want to, if that's what you mean," she snapped, brushing past him with little care that she might jostle them both out of the tree.

"Would you do his work, though?" He didn't want to inflame her resentment, but he couldn't stop his tongue. The dread of the last few moments seemed to be shaking out of him in petty spite. Perhaps it was just another color of fear.

"I don't even know what his work is!" She whirled her face up toward him. "But my mother is a midwife, and I'm not ashamed of anything she has taught me. She eases pain and heals sick folk and helps babies come into the world without killing their mothers on the way. Most of the time, anyway."

"Does your mother stop babies from being born, too?" he asked. "That's a sin, witch or not."

The storm on her face held back her words while she kept climbing down. When they had both settled their feet again on the earth, Aidan reached for Lana's arm. He meant to appease her anger and his own trepidation with a reminder of what mattered now.

"Listen—"

She jerked away. "No! Spare me your sermon! If you were a girl, and you had ever been raped, you would not think my mother's work such a sin!"

Shock bound them both for an instant. Lana whirled to cover her face with her hands and then flatten them against the oak's trunk as if borrowing strength.

Aidan drew a few difficult breaths, trying to seal his foolish mouth, but he couldn't stand to leave her words dangling in the air between them. The look on her face was too raw. He touched her elbow.

"Lana . . . ?"

Her eyes flicked to him darkly, then away. Those wounded eyes answered the question in his mind. He wanted to tell her he was sorry, but it seemed the useless words would only prolong a painful blaze he wished he had never kindled.

She crossed her arms tightly and turned, her face closed. "Never mind."

"Let's get away from here," he sighed, starting off. Lana did not follow.

"Wait," she said. "This tree sheltered us without being properly asked. I need to thank it."

Raising his eyebrows, he stepped back. "How are you going to do that?" He half expected her to launch into some deranged dance or call in some spirit. He wouldn't stop her, because they would surely be dead if they had not climbed that tree, but a tremor of worry coursed the back of his neck.

She cast about nearby. She found a few white pebbles and a small patch of wood violet. Aidan watched while she plucked a flower and arranged it with the stones at the base of the tree. When she was done, she tipped her head to gaze into the tree's branches and whispered, "For Aidan and me. 'Gratitude for wood and bough, for haven given us just now.'" She rose, casting him a baleful glance.

"Gratitude," he repeated, nodding. He released a tense breath, relieved that a verse he'd heard before had been her only incantation.

They slipped silently through the forest again. They began more carefully than before, Lana pausing several times to work her hazel rod. But being constantly alert was exhausting, and the rod did not point out danger again. As the hour waned, Aidan hoped the raiders would either be hunkering down for the evening or, better yet, leaving before the afternoon light dwindled.

"Is this hiding place much farther?" he asked.

"Not too far," she said. "It'll be a good place for the night. You'll see."

Aidan didn't answer. He resolved to stash her away, if her choice seemed as safe as she said, and then return to sneak up on the abbey once the sun set. He had to find out if Rory and brothers Eamon and Nathan and the others were safe. If so, he could collect Lana again and they could both slip inside the guardian wall.

"I'm sorry I made you angry before," he said, after a moment.

"When you told me you could hear numbers," she said, "I didn't ask if you were crazy."

Heat rose into his scalp. "I don't think it is really the same," he ventured.

"Yes, it is," she replied. "You hear something most people don't: the secret sounds of numbers hidden inside everything. I can feel and . . . and draw out the secrets hidden in trees. We both know some secrets. The only difference I can see, really, is that I have someone who can show me how to use what I've learned about trees."

He watched his feet, trying to find some flaw in her comparison. "Maybe you're right," he allowed.

"Have you told Father Niall or the other monks that you hear numbers?" she asked.

"Only one," Aidan admitted.

When he didn't elaborate, Lana cast him a smug look. "I suppose he thought it was the Devil's voice?"

"What if it is?" he said, low and almost to himself.

"Nonsense. Do the numbers you hear tell you to hurt anyone?"

Aidan dragged in a thick breath and shook his head.

The humming did not direct him to do anything at all. When he had been younger, it had helped him know whom to doubt and whom to rely on, when to keep his thoughts to himself, or where to turn for advice. He had used it the same way a whiff of food told him whether a bite would taste sweet, bitter, or savory. Since becoming a monk, however, and the unpleasant conversation with Brother Eamon, Aidan had grown hesitant to even acknowledge the humming.

Though she did not appear to need convincing, he said, "I tell myself that God made the numbers and everything else, so He must make them hum."

"Well, it certainly cannot be the Devil if it causes no harm," she declared. "And I should know, since you have decided that I am an expert in the Devil's work."

A chuckle and a groan left Aidan together. He protested, "You're angry with me for something I never said."

"Your face said it for you."

Unable to deny that, he stayed silent.

A few paces later, she wondered, "Do you hear numbers from trees, too?"

"In the twenties, usually," he replied, relieved that the annoyance had faded from her voice. "Although willows hum thirty-one. Things that love water almost always have numbers with threes."

Thoughtful, she fingered her lips. Aidan looked away quickly. Some inarticulate force inside him persisted in wondering what those lips felt like to touch.

When her hand dropped to release another question, he expected her to ask more about trees. As usual, Lana surprised him.

"What's your number, Aidan?"

He could not answer. The numbers spoke to him, not of him. He must also have a hum, he supposed, but he couldn't hear it.

"Don't you know?" she pressed.

He shook his head.

She canted her chin, gazing sideways at him. A smile played her lips. "I think you're a five."

He looked over sharply, afraid she was mocking.

"Is that bad?" she added, at his reaction. "I'm just guessing. Do you want to be a twelve so you're higher than me?"

Bewildered amusement pushed a laugh from his chest.

"It doesn't work like that." The idea that he might be a twelve was even more ridiculous than the idea that a higher number carried more worth. Except for the unpleasant number one, which Aidan associated with turmoil, different numbers were only different, not better. They all had failings and strengths.

"Well, what are you, then?"

Aidan puffed out his cheeks, feeling pressured to answer. He stopped walking and exhaled. As the air flowed out of his body, he closed his eyes and stilled his thoughts. He tried not to inhale again for a long time, paused there at the bottom of breathing. He didn't expect to hear any hum from inside, nor did he. But he thought of others he knew and traits common to people with the same numbers, and he tried to find himself in the patterns. Some numbers were easy to dismiss. Five was tempting, however. His father—

A cramp of dread disrupted Aidan's thoughts. *If his father was still alive,* that dread whispered, *and not lying cold amid a muddle of ashes and blood.* He forced his mind forward past that image: His father was a five, and Aidan would be proud to share that number.

"You know," he told Lana, opening his eyes, "you might be right about five. I hope so." He regarded her.

She did not smirk or speak, merely returned his gaze. Those blue eyes tickled him. He squirmed.

"Do you hear them, too?" he asked softly. "The numbers, I mean?" He felt naked before her.

She only smiled and reached for his hand.

Aidan stiffened, wary but entranced. He did not pull away. They'd traveled hand in hand for much of their flight, but this contact felt different. It felt secret. Afraid to know that secret, Aidan averted his gaze. He pondered the courage and responsibility, the stubbornness and hot temper and occasional dullness of five-ish folk he had known, and he refused to think about linked fingers at all.

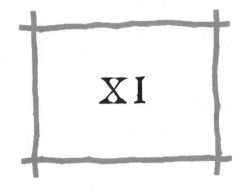

XI

The land beneath them began rising, and they veered into a gully that Aidan recognized. They had circled around north of the abbey and now passed not far from the local beekeeper's cottage. Aidan began planning the shortest route back toward the abbey, mapping a course in his head. Though he craned his neck looking, no gaps in the greenery gave him more than a glimpse toward it, nor any hint of what may have transpired there.

As a breeze drifted past, Aidan froze. Lana stumbled, brought up short by their linked hands.

"What is it?" she whimpered, crowding close to clutch him. "Did you hear something?" She fumbled with her hazel rod.

Aidan breathed deeply, all senses flaring. He couldn't hear the humming of any number low enough to come from a person, but he didn't trust that. His instincts had stopped him, not his mind, and he wasn't sure why. Perhaps another troop of skulking raiders was just a little too distant to hear. For that matter, perhaps Norsemen had no numbers. He had refused even to listen during the passing of the previous band. Now he regretted that cowardly impulse.

As he scoured the undergrowth for motion, Aidan resisted the urge to flee for cover. If some enemy lurked, the hare's trick of remaining frozen and silent might serve them better now.

"I don't feel any danger close by," Lana whispered, lowering her divining stick.

A dab of red drew Aidan's eye. He realized what had set off his internal alarm. Some of the tension left his limbs, and he drew his hand loose from hers.

"I smell blood," he said softly, "which means there must be a lot. Stay here." He stepped carefully forward to investigate.

Ignoring his instruction, she crept along at his heels. They slipped between trees and shortly Aidan could follow his eyes instead of his nose. Something bleeding had passed through the woods, leaving splatters of darkening red on leaves and the earth. The number and size of the stains made him wonder how far the one bleeding could possibly have gotten.

They soon reached the clearing around the beekeeper's house. Thick-bodied bees crisscrossed the meadow, their drone filling the air. Their hollow logs and straw hives sat in clusters among the clover, apparently undisturbed. After long, silent study, Aidan decided the house offered no threat.

"Let's go," Lana urged, looking over both of her shoulders. "Nobody's here."

"I told you to stay back there," he countered. "I shouldn't be long. There still may be someone alive here who needs help."

He slipped across the yard. Once he rounded a corner of the house, the source of the scent lay in plain sight. A horse sprawled on the ground, the soil churned into red mud by the animal's death throes and great gushes of blood. Its wounds leaked yet, but enough time had passed that ravens had begun showing interest. Neither the sight nor the cloying tang in Aidan's nose was much different from what he knew from slaughtering cattle, but the greater violence and disarray turned his stomach.

Hoof prints and more blood trailed away from the trampled earth and back the direction he had come. Glad to turn away from the carcass, Aidan visually traced that path to the trees where Lana fidgeted. She gestured anxiously when she saw him look back. Signaling for her to wait yet, he turned and explored a bit farther.

The gate to the animal pen stood wide open. The livestock it should have confined had escaped or been taken as spoils. The beekeeper was not to be found, either. He may have fled on the second, wounded horse, but he'd more likely been captured, perhaps by the same raiders who had come back down the hill with a prisoner in tow. Either way, the man had not gone without a fight. A dead Viking lay near the door to the cottage.

Drawn, Aidan crept near enough to peer into the enemy's face. With a choked cry, he leapt back. The attacker was not dead yet after all. An almost inaudible humming rose from him.

Keeping well beyond the reach of any sudden movement, Aidan stared. The fallen Viking neither twitched nor opened his eyes. Although mortally wounded, he had not yet been claimed by the fatal blow—a hunting javelin plunged through the barrel of his chest.

Aidan let the man's weak sound of three fill his ears. So Norsemen, too, had numbers. Troubled that this dread enemy's near-corpse hummed of the same number as several of his childhood friends, Aidan wondered if the man had shared their quick humor and staunch loyalty. He rather hoped the Vikings' numbers, as well as their mouths, spoke a different language. Unfortunately for his peace of mind, the men he knew who hummed of three were quick on their feet, not easily frightened, good with weapons, and enthusiastic hunters. At least one had rustled cattle from distant rivals, and all of Aidan's three-ish friends might have made passable raiders.

The squawk of a feasting bird split the air. Startled, Aidan glanced around. The Norsemen might come back for this fallen comrade before they departed.

"What took so long? What were you doing?" hissed Lana, when he hurried back to her.

"Trying to figure out what happened."

"Was anyone inside the cottage?"

Aidan gripped her arm and drew her away through the trees back the way they had come. She took his silence as a negative answer.

As the beekeeper's house receded behind foliage and shadows, Aidan regretted not taking the javelin or checking for any food there to scavenge. He'd become distracted by the dying Viking, and that lapse filled him with shame. Briefly he considered returning. It would be best, he decided, to hide Lana and then go to learn if the abbey, or anywhere else, was safe yet. He hoped neither of them would need a weapon.

"Which way to your hiding spot?" he asked, realizing that he'd taken the lead. "If it is near here, it might not be very safe. They may return."

"This way," she said, adjusting their course. "And 'tis not so close as that. But tell me, Aidan, what did you see back there?"

"A dead horse and an almost-dead raider," he said.

"Almost?" Her voice slanted up to nervous heights.

" 'Tis all right," he assured her. "He'll be dead soon enough. I could only tell that he wasn't because I could still hear his humming."

"Like a heartbeat?" Lana asked, surprised.

"A little, I suppose," he said, "if you could play different heartbeats like different notes on a pipe."

They hurried onward, their distance from the bloody yard growing. Hearing a nearby trickling of water, Lana said, "I'm thirsty. Could we get a drink?"

He agreed and they ducked under branches and parted brush until they reached the small stream. Lana sank onto her knees with a sigh to scoop water with her hands. Once Aidan also had quenched his thirst, she remained on the ground. He crouched down beside her.

"Tired?" he asked.

She rolled her head in an awkward no, not wanting to admit it but not lying very well. He wondered how she'd managed to fool any pilgrims.

"I can hear that you are," he said gently. "You need not be ashamed. We can rest here a minute."

"Mostly I'm frightened," she sighed. "But that's making me feel worn-out."

Aidan felt similarly, but as he hunkered near her, he tried to keep his eyes on the forest around them, alert to the rustling and life there.

"Do your ears get tired?" Lana asked.

Confused, Aidan blinked. At first he thought she meant listening for danger. Then he realized she was still poking into his sense of the numbers.

He shrugged. "Some numbers are more pleasant than others. But usually they all meld together into a sound like the rush of the river. I ignore it a lot of the time."

She caressed her hazel rod between her hands.

"When I'm crafting a wood charm, I can feel the energy of the wood in my hands—a vibration, almost. Do you think it might be the same thing?"

Aidan drew a long breath, fighting a swell of annoyance. He had already explained more about the numbers to her than he had ever consciously laid out for himself. He managed to keep his voice soft as he replied, "You keep asking me questions I don't know the answers to, Lana."

"I'm sorry. I just want to understand."

Her eleven filled the silence between them, hushed and sunken in her fatigue. Aidan could nonetheless hear within it a note of burning curiosity that defined her. Raising his eyes, he saw that she still awaited an answer, and with more than curiosity in her face. There was some barter going on here under the surface, a trade he did not understand. As that recognition flared within him, it kindled both apprehension and thrill. He found he wanted to bargain with her, blind though it felt.

Nibbling at his fingers, he let his gaze course the stream bank, looking for something that might help him satisfy her.

"Close your eyes for a moment," he told Lana, "and hold out your hands."

A fleeting distrust crossed her face, but she set her hazel rod in her lap and lifted her hands.

He turned her hands palms up and cupped them together. When he glanced higher to check that her eyelids had closed, a small paralysis gripped him. He crouched there, unable to let go of her hands, while his eyes mapped her lashes, the sturdy strokes of her brows, and the delicate veins in her eyelids. He couldn't remember ever having looked so closely at someone who was not looking back, and he liked it. Then the curve of her cheek shaded more pink than it had been a moment before and her eyes began to twitch under their lids. Alarmed by a similar flutter in his chest, Aidan released her hands and stood up.

"Just stay like that for a moment," he said. "I'm only stepping away to pick something up."

Aidan scooped a handful of waterworn pebbles from the shallows of the stream. He dropped two into Lana's outstretched hands.

"Without looking, how many rocks in your hands?"

She curled her palms to feel. "Two."

He slipped in a few more. "And now?"

Her next reply took a bit longer and wasn't as sure. "Seven?"

He dumped the rest he had gathered into her hands. "Now?"

A gentle snort escaped her. "I would have to hold them against me and pluck them from one hand to the other to count."

"My numbers are rather like that," Aidan said.

She opened her eyes. "That is feeling, not hearing. You said you heard them."

Aidan battled exasperation. "I do, Lana! But that's as close as I can explain. What I hear is a sound, but I feel the number inside it. Like . . . you can hear someone hollering from a distance, but you have to be closer to make out the words. And if it is a high number, I need time and concentration to get it."

Lana must have heard the frustration in his voice. She deposited the pebbles on the ground. "Thank you for trying so hard to explain it," she murmured, without looking up.

Ashamed of his impatience with her, Aidan said, "I've never really talked about it before." He meant to help excuse his ineptness, but once his words lay in the air, they seemed to say more about loneliness.

Lana's eyes found his and lingered, her gaze disconcerting without conversation to help interpret it. The color of deep water, those eyes pulled at him. Aidan found himself wanting to respond by telling her more things he'd never told anyone else.

"We should go," he said softly instead, realizing how long they'd been motionless and astray from their purpose. "It is not safe to stay here in the open and talk as if nothing has happened."

Still silent, she nodded. He helped her to her feet.

Aidan gestured at the hazel rod, which Lana had been careful not to forget. "Do you want to try that again?" he asked. "Just in case?"

A surprised look lit her face. She agreed. Once she had satisfied herself that no danger loomed imminently, they started walking again.

Shortly Lana said, "Can I ask one more question, Aidan?"

Caught for an instant between anger and laughter, he opted for the latter and nodded.

"You told me before you had never heard a person with a number as high as mine." Her brow creased in anxiety. "Do you think there might be something wrong with me?"

"No," he reassured her, but her question recalled the odd hum of one that he heard from Rory, and how that number did not seem to fit his young friend. Wondering if she had a point, he cast for memories that might provide clues. A grin broke through his sober thoughts.

"Although I will tell you," he added, "that before I met you, I think I only heard eleven from cats."

"Oh! I don't know if I like that or not!"

"I doubt it means too much. You just have the same kind of . . . lazy mystery."

"Lazy?" Affronted, she reached to slap at his arm.

"And fierce claws!" he added, laughing. "And intense curiosity and eerie eyes and graceful movements and—" Feeling himself stumbling into dangerous territory, he shifted focus quickly. "I don't know if the number comes from the traits or the traits come from the number. I have just learned to match them up over the years."

"Fine," she said, in a mock huff. "I can be aloof like a cat, too."

While she pretended to sulk, Aidan pondered, intrigued by the puzzle Lana had raised.

"I have wondered why people hum of the lowest numbers," he admitted. "I think it might be because people are closer to God. And everything else in the world, everything with numbers higher than ten, is more connected to . . . well, everything else. So their numbers multiply with each other somehow."

"So eleven is farther from God than everyone else?" Her voice, trembling, revealed that she was trying hard not to be hurt.

Aidan took a deep breath, searching for the right thing to say.

"No," he replied quietly. "I didn't mean that. And I am

only guessing; I surely don't know. But I don't think your eleven is bad, Lana. I think you're just a little more connected to the rest of the world."

He peeked sidelong at her, loath to see insult or annoyance on her face. She kept her gaze firmly fixed on the forest floor.

He bit his lip, then added, "I like hearing eleven."

Her eyes flashed to him, but for only an instant. Sorry he'd said more than was needed, Aidan tucked his hands into the opposite sleeves and bowed his head. He saw a new value in the monks' rule of silence.

They each traveled in their own thoughts until Lana alerted him to the end of their journey at last.

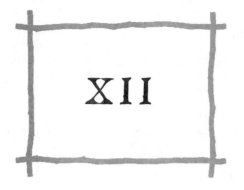

XII

Lana led Aidan to a grove of old trees on a steep side of the hill. When he saw a large snag that had rotted away at the base, leaving a hollow, he pointed.

"Is that where you mean to hide?" The foxhole was large enough and sheltered from weather, but anyone walking past would see them curled inside.

"No. That makes my place better, because nobody would look farther than that." She ducked past the snag and picked her way to another nearby giant. Battered by lightning or wind some years ago, the tree had uprooted and fallen. The cluster of broken roots at its base now arched high over their heads, splayed and curled like the legs of a spider. Rowan and ivy had taken root in mossy crevices between the uplifted roots, and saplings piggy-backed all along the half-rotten trunk.

"Flying rowan, that's called, since it does not take root

in the earth," Lana said, pointing to the green rowan sprays over their heads. "If I wanted to make a flying switch, so I could fly back home without fear of the raiders, that is what I would use."

Aidan looked from the rowan to Lana, resisting the impulse to sidle away from her.

She rolled her eyes. "I'm teasing, for goodness' sake. If anyone can really fly by riding a branch, I haven't learned how."

Aware that rowan was nonetheless sometimes called witch-wood, he asked, "Is that what you were trying to sell to the pilgrims?" When the abbot had asked where her false relics had come from, she had said that a tree sprite had shown her where to find them. Now, Aidan could almost believe it.

His question dispelled her playful smile. "That wood is nothing I know, Aidan. That's why I wanted it back. I was only trying to sell it because I was hungry."

Her words filled him with sympathy and frustration. He hated feeling so powerless, and he had never suffered it with such impatience as he did in her presence. He resolved to mend that discomfort with action as soon as he could.

She led him nearer the upthrust wall of roots. A hawthorn shrub crowded the arch between two splayed roots and the trunk.

Hawthorn, hagthorn, bush of May,
Unlock your thorns for us today.

After reciting those lines, Lana reached to the hawthorn and drew aside a spiked branch. A passage lay behind it where the downed tree's enormous roots humped up from the ground, holding the fallen trunk in the air and leaving an arched hollow beneath them. Clotted dirt and more roots formed a back wall deeper inside. From outside the hawthorn, the tree cave was invisible from every direction.

"Duck down," she said. "And mind the thorns. It doesn't know you." She slipped under the cruel branch and disappeared into the dead tree's huge root ball.

The hawthorn sprang back into place. Aidan tried to brush it out of the way and promptly stuck himself.

"Ouch."

The branches shivered and parted. Lana's face and hand appeared.

"Move more slowly. Come on." She held the branch for him, backing in her crouch as he entered. The thorns caught his robe on all sides, but with her help he eased past.

Once inside, Aidan straightened cautiously. The nook extended almost his height at its peak. Nearly as wide, it ranged deep enough so that a cow could have sheltered there comfortably. Daylight filtered in through the hawthorn. His eyes took a moment to adjust to the murk, but when they did, he saw that Lana had been here before. Candle stubs rested in a small wooden bowl stashed among the twisted roots. The dirt and crumbling rot under their feet had been spread with fern fronds, and a long-wilted daisy chain hung from a notch in the wood. Aidan only hoped that none of the humped roots supporting the tree's weight would choose today to settle deeper in rot.

"If we had a flint and char I could light the candles," Lana said. "But we don't." She perched on a knob of root-wood curving out as if for that purpose. "I've never been here at night, but I won't be too scared with you here. I know we're safe from people, at least."

"This is a good hiding spot," Aidan agreed. He took a deep breath, trying to ignore a sudden reluctance to be separated from her. "But I'm going to leave you here safe by yourself for a while. It will be dark soon, and I've got to find out what has happened at the abbey and see if it is wise for us to return yet."

"No! Don't leave me!"

Her plea dug at him. He gritted his teeth, reminding himself she would be far safer here than with him.

"If the abbey's secure," he promised, "I'll come back to get you."

"What if you meet them again in the woods? And what if you can't find your way back in the dark? And what if the abbey's *not* safe? They might see you coming!"

Aidan dropped to his haunches before her. "Lana, I can't just hide here with you, not knowing. I'll—"

"Why not?"

"Because." He floundered for a better answer, and added, "If the Norsemen are still here, the survivors and any of your father's men who escaped will be mustering to fight back. They'll need anyone they can get. Like me."

"You're a monk! What do you know about fighting?"

"As much as any other commoner," Aidan said, pushing back a hot flush of defensiveness. "I'll be back for you as soon as I can."

"But—" She stopped. Aidan could read the question in her eyes anyway.

"If I don't come back," he replied gently, "you'd better wait another full day before you come look, or at least until you're so hungry you don't have any choice. They won't stay forever."

"Aidan!" The fright in her voice tore at his skin.

"You'll be all right," he told her, trying to convince both of them. Though his head assured him this plan was best, his heart argued. Feeling his determination waver, Aidan turned to duck out before it failed completely. He hoped the hawthorn gate would let him go more easily than it had admitted him.

"Wait. Take this."

When he looked back over his shoulder, she drew her

red yarn necklace over her head. The crossed twigs tied at its center were wound with a separate length of red wool.

"Your cross? Why?"

She rose to drape it over his head and tuck the bits of wood down the neck of his robe. Her touch, too familiar to be polite, made Aidan's skin tingle. He jigged nervously.

"It is not just a cross," she said, not meeting his eyes. "'Tis my charm from the flying rowan I showed you outside. 'Twill help protect you. Are the oak leaves still here or did they fall out?" She patted his chest.

Aidan opened his mouth to protest her motherly fussing, raising a hand to push hers away. Before he could, she found the leaves snagged in the wool of his robe. Her palm flattened there and she shifted closer, raising her eyes. Suddenly her touch didn't feel so motherly. The hand Aidan had lifted to remove hers only curled around her fingers instead. He could feel his heart beating hard beneath both of their hands.

"Lana," Aidan murmured, unsure what words would follow.

"Be careful," she said. She tipped her face down toward their hands, but he saw her cheeks bloom. "Come back." Though she didn't look up, an impish grin appeared through her blush. "You still have to teach me to read."

That grin was worse than her blush. Never in his life

had Aidan wanted to kiss someone so badly. He hadn't had much practice, and the scant kissing he had tried in the past had brought him more guilty thrill than pleasure. It had felt a bit sloppy and dangerous, as if drool might intrude at any instant. Kissing Lana would be different. He could tell by the hot tingling between them. It felt like the breathless moment between lightning and thunder.

Aidan closed his eyes, protecting himself from the pull of her lips. His face cramped in struggle. When he opened his eyes, he had remembered that he was a monk. Not a good monk; a good monk would have let go of her hand and moved away. Aidan let go of her hand to graze her jaw with his fingertips in wordless longing.

That proved to be a mistake. Lana's face tipped upward under his hand and as her eyes struck his, Aidan's mind stopped working at all. Without his meaning it, his hand curled to better fit her jaw, drawing her face closer. His lips met hers. She gasped delicately, and he felt the tiny intake of breath tug at him, moving his body to lean into hers.

Lana kissed him in return, and Aidan would have forgotten the abbey and the Vikings and everything else if she hadn't drawn away after a long, fiery moment. Her palm, still flat on his chest, pushed back with increasing pressure until finally he felt it. He caught himself. When he again opened his eyes, unaware of when they had closed, she was staring at him, her own eyes drawn wide. Now her hand leapt away from his heart as if burned.

Aidan drew a ragged breath. His chest ached and pounded as though he'd been running.

"I didn't mean to do that," he mumbled, more to himself than to her.

"I don't mind that you did." Her cheeks blazing, Lana's gaze fell away. Her fluttering fingers twisted in a lock of her hair. Somewhere she'd lost the length of yarn that had bound it.

"I shouldn't have."

"Why not?"

Aidan ran both hands through his hair and turned to go. Her question was too vast for him to even scratch at the answer.

"I'll be back," he said, thickly.

"After that, you had better," she said, her lips crushing a smile. The smile blinked out. "I might not have anyone else left."

Her plaintive words snagged Aidan's heart. Images of burnt-out cottages and dead bodies filled his head and he turned back to her once more, in part to banish those thoughts.

"Here," he said, dropping to one knee. He shoved

aside the fern fronds and drew four figures in the soft duff below: **ᚪ ᛒ ᚳ ᚦ**.

"Ah, bay, kay, dhay," he said as he drew. "The first four Latin letters." He ran through their main sounds and added, "Learn them while I'm gone." Without waiting for any reaction or letting himself be snared again by her eyes, he shoved through the hawthorn and escaped, oblivious to the scratches he took from the thorns.

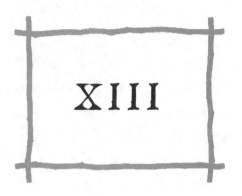

XIII

Aidan revisited that kiss the entire way back through the woods. What stunned him most was not how hopelessly unchaste it had been or the way he could still feel her lips against his. The shocking thing was the number that had hummed behind that kiss. He could close his eyes and retrieve it, a deep bass emptiness—not nothing, but None. Different from the soundless nothing of sleep or the chill draft from an unoccupied grave, this Naught seared a white-hot blank against darkness, a thrumming so low he heard it in his bones. None vibrated of floods, of clearing away, of transformation and change. None was the sound of the full moon and the round sun breaking over the eastern horizon. It was the sound, Aidan imagined, that the heavens had made on the first day, before God had done anything more than move upon the face of the waters. If it wasn't blasphemy to think such a thing, it was very nearly the humming of the Lord God Himself.

His amazement was quenched by the sudden realization that he wasn't sure where he was. Returning back through the woods in the twilight proved harder than Aidan had guessed. Though already aloft, the lopsided moon danced too often with clouds to offer much aid. Stumbling onto a clearing in the trees, Aidan made out enough of the terrain below to reorient himself. Twice more, however, he found himself confronting a creek in the wrong place or a hill where he'd expected a hollow. Only after he gave up on his eyes to follow the stench of burning and the slope under his feet did he finally aim true.

Eventually he broke into open fields and got his bearings. Then Aidan coursed the drystone walls, moving in long Z shapes toward the monastery. It blotted the horizon like black ink splashed on a purple drape. The evening was dreadfully silent, free from the grunting of pigs and the braying of donkeys. A few orange streaks in the distance marked roofs and crops still smoldering yet. Aidan stayed hunched in the shelter of the low walls, not stopping to prod any of the lumpy shadows in the fields. They were clearly not cattle or sheep. He did not want to recognize more than that.

When he drew near the abbey's rear gate, he hunkered under a tree for a long while, listening to nothing and seeing even less. He smelled char but could not find a billow of smoke. If anyone at all breathed inside the monastery's ramparts, it was not apparent.

Aidan crept to the gate, which he found ajar. Peering through the gap revealed more darkness. Drawing a tense breath, he slipped inside.

He dropped immediately to a crouch, nearly invisible alongside the thick gatepost. Robed bodies, impossible to deny, were strewn in the yard.

Aidan swallowed hard against the gorge that rose in his throat. Cowls and hems fluttered, lifted by the light night-time breeze. Their owners no longer hummed of numbers at all. Aidan could hear only faint echoes, mostly the desperation of one, bouncing in the yard's vast, hollow silence.

He scanned the nearest building, the kitchen. No light glowed from inside. When he was sure that this much of the compound, at least, was deserted, he crept toward the Great Hall and the monks' cells beyond. The minutes dragged with his feet. He bit his tongue to keep from calling out for one of his brethren, anyone, to answer. The only thought that kept him from fleeing was the recognition that the corpses on display were not enough to account for all of the monks. The rest could be holed up or hostages yet.

The rows of monks' cells and the novices' dormitory also were still. In the yard between there and the front gate, Aidan froze. He feared he recognized a slight form sprawled in the dust. After long seconds, motionless except for the thudding of his heart, Aidan goaded himself to check closer. Once he had already decided whose body it must be, he could finally move his feet.

Rory had fallen facedown. Wincing, Aidan put a hand on his shoulder to gently roll him. He whimpered at the result. His friend had been struck across the back of the neck with a heavy blade. His broken neck had been nearly severed as well, so Rory's body flopped over while his head only lolled. Aidan's stomach lurched. Empty, it had nothing to discharge but bitter phlegm.

Not hearing his own sobbing breath, he gently pushed Rory's body back into place. He hoped the younger boy had not seen the blow coming, but his sprawl suggested he had been running. Aidan doubted that the foreknowledge of a short life had much eased Rory's fear at its end. His eyes burned at that thought. He didn't bother, in the dark, to blink away the gathering tears.

When Aidan lifted his hand from Rory's shoulder, his palm squelched, sticky. Revolted, he leapt back to his feet. Furiously scrubbing his bloody hand across the wool of his robe, he dashed blindly toward the abbey's main gate. He'd seen enough.

A bell rang.

Startled beyond reason, Aidan plastered himself against

the nearest refuge, the High Cross that loomed near the gate. It offered no comfort but the cover of shadow. His mind flailed to connect the ringing with the fact that the monastery seemed to be peopled with nothing but corpses. The bell had tolled four times before he realized it was not random noise but the steady, sedate mark of the hours. Seven chimes altogether, calling monks to the evening's last prayers as though nothing had happened.

Half expecting the dead to rise and answer that call, Aidan did not. He only pressed his limbs tighter to the carved cross. Both the stone and cold sweat chilled his body before the obvious truth wormed into his mind: Somebody in the abbey still lived.

His muscles suddenly mobile again, he hurried back the way he had come. He remembered something he'd considered earlier and, in the horror of corpses, forgotten: Any of his brethren who had outpaced or outwitted the raiders could be hunkered in the souterrain, an underground tunnel used most of the time for food storage. Its entrance near the kitchen garden was hidden, this time of year, by berry brambles run wild. Of course that's where survivors would be. He should have gone there first.

Rounding a corner of the Great Hall at a run, he saw the darkness ahead flicker and thin. Perhaps a dozen hooded figures, lit lamps in hand, were emerging from the earth as if from a grave. At the sound of his racing footsteps, they froze. His heart jerking, Aidan skidded to a halt, too. He'd seen the same figures, with the same glow about them, every night since he'd become a novice. Never before, though, had he heard the fearsome drone of the number one around them. With that sound grating behind his jaw, those walking shadows too easily could be ghosts.

Aidan only caught his breath again when he recognized Brother Eamon.

"Brother Aidan. Praise be to Him," Eamon murmured, coming out of the gloom. His face looked haggard. "How is it that God has spared you? I thought you'd been taken or slain."

"I was outside the walls, in the woods," Aidan explained, "on an errand for Brother Nathan. The attack—how did it happen?"

Eamon lowered his head and moved forward once more. Aidan fell in alongside him. A few more monks, apparently the first to quit the tunnel, approached from other directions. Aidan spotted Brother Nathan's sharp profile a few dark figures ahead. It was he who had rung the handbell; it still dangled in his grip.

"They were inside the gate swinging swords without warning," Brother Eamon told Aidan. "We were caught unawares. They gave no quarter and no chance to ransom our safety by paying a tribute. And clearly our blessed

Saint Nevin did not intervene on behalf of his monks." He shook his head, his face wrenched with sorrow. "I fear our youngest brothers suffered the most. Many were near the gate in a game of rounders and stood amazed for too long before starting to run. Every novice—every one except you—was taken captive or killed."

"I saw Brother Rory," Aidan murmured.

Eamon sighed. "The abbot fell also, trying to stop some of the plunder. Other brave martyrs drew attention from our tunnel. But though a few of us hid from the heathens, God's wrath has still found us. We must have strayed from the path Christ intended."

Aidan blinked, not understanding. The elder monk made it sound as if the attack had been somehow deserved.

"How many brothers are left?" he asked. Surely this dozen were only a part. "And what's going on? Why did the bell toll?"

"The bell?" Brother Eamon echoed. He nodded toward the altar as they entered the chapel. "It is the Hour of Compline. We must pray."

"Now?"

When his mentor cast him a chiding look, Aidan added, "Bodies lie everywhere. Can we not at least bring them in and lay them to rest?"

Brother Eamon's sagging face hardened.

"The dead will not wander away, Brother Aidan," he said. "Our duty first is to God."

Aidan's feet stopped while he fumbled for a response. Eamon kept walking.

"The gates, though—the rear gate was unguarded," Aidan argued. "I came in that way. What if the raiders come back?"

The monk walking just behind him, a sour-faced stone-cutter Aidan generally avoided, stepped around him and said, "Look about, novice. The heathens have small reason to return. There is naught left to defile."

Locked in place while the remaining monks flowed about him, Aidan lifted his eyes. The chapel had been brutalized. The communion chalice and the fine fabrics dressing the altar were gone, along with the bronze crucifix that had hung over it and the gold candlesticks alongside. The silver censers had been torn from their chains, the carved wooden reliquaries hacked open. The old monk who had tended them slumped nearby, also hacked open, having apparently tried to protect the bones of Saint Nevin. Those remains lay scattered ingloriously, of little value to heathens. The more worldly relics, a jeweled girdle and other effects of the saint, had vanished.

A weight hit Aidan's heart along with a new realization—the manuscripts, too, had surely been stolen. Certainly the books that belonged on the altar and lectern were missing.

"The scriptorium?" he moaned. He darted to Brother Nathan, near the front of the procession. At Aidan's touch on his sleeve, the monk granted the novice a kindly look out of place on his usually strict features.

"You have cheated the Angel of Death, Brother Aidan," he said. "Would that I had sent a dozen novices after oak apples today."

"The books, Brother Nathan—are they gone?" Even the profane books in the collection, copies of Greek verse and philosophy, counted among the monastery's most priceless possessions. Neither those nor the holy works could be read or valued by heathens, but the pirates weren't fools. Royals and nobles and, shamefully, other monasteries across Éire, Britannia, and Gaul would pay handsomely, no questions asked, to possess them.

"I fear it is so," Nathan said. "I have just come from there. The bound volumes were ravaged or stolen, the loose folios and wood tablets burned. I did not dare collect any before retreating to the tunnel. In cowardice I have sinned." He drew a hand over his long face.

Aidan squirmed in unfamiliar sympathy for a man who had previously caused him only awe. Meekly, he protested, "God could not blame you for wanting to live, could He?"

"Do not presume to know the Holy mind, novice," Brother Nathan said, the sharpness returning to his voice.

Automatically, Aidan recoiled to whisper, "Forgive me."

Brother Nathan's lips curled in a rueful smile. "It is not my place to forgive you. I particularly would not presume to forgive you today. I half expected to hear your confession upon your return. I feared the mundane world would tempt you. Thus my pride and arrogance are revealed, it would seem. I never guessed you would return to hear mine."

Aidan dropped his eyes, clamping his teeth on his tongue and feeling disoriented. When he looked back up, Nathan had stepped to the lectern. With the abbot dead, the scriptorium's master was the senior monk until another abbot could be chosen. Staring over Aidan's head, he took a deep breath and chanted the first lines of a prayer that, though familiar, seemed ironic tonight: "O God, come to my aid: O Lord, hasten to help me." The worship had begun.

"Take your place, Brother Aidan," muttered Brother Eamon, who alone had moved up behind him in the aisle. The remaining monks had filed into their usual places. The chapel looked mournfully empty. Aidan shivered as Nathan's voice echoed, then paused, most likely awaiting his retreat.

"Given the day's events, your confusion can be overlooked," Eamon added. "But you have been out of obedience long enough."

As he turned in response, Aidan's gaze slid to the

novices' corner of the chapel. Its blankness mocked him. His features twisted in dismay, and he ran a hand through his hair as if it could comb away the snarls inside him. Rory should be standing in that blank space, trying to hide his usual smirk. Aidan's skin crawled at the memory of the lifeless, unturning head. Here in the lamp glow he could see Rory's gore tracked across his own chest, and the sight ignited his heart. It burned in resentment toward a God who had planned Rory's death well enough to warn him, but not well enough to include a more compassionate or at least comprehensible alternative in His grand design.

Straightening, Aidan cast his eyes back again on the bare altar, the crushed reliquaries, and Brother Nathan's drawn face. It all looked and felt wrong. More important, it *sounded* wrong. He had grown accustomed to the numbers that always hummed through the chapel under the chanting, the mingling vibrations of monks and song and devotion. He'd been so often engulfed in them, reverberating in the hollows of his mind, that he had stopped hearing them. Now they had changed—or Aidan's hearing had simply grown clearer. The chapel's numbers were no longer complex harmonies of dutiful sixes, reverent eights, vibrant threes, and inspired nines. Now they were grim ones and twos overlaid with the slick whine of seven.

His stomach churning at the disharmony, Aidan turned

back to Brother Eamon. He did not dare meet the elder monk's eyes. The order to take his usual place still hung in the air.

"No," he whispered, trying the word in his heart. He could not stand in this discordant chapel and worship while Rory's corpse still sprawled in the dirt.

"Brother Aidan." The warning was terse. Aidan knew he would not get another.

He swallowed and looked Brother Eamon in the face. "No," he repeated, harder, before he turned and walked out.

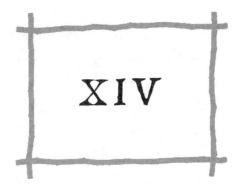

XIV

When he lifted Rory's limp body, Aidan took great care to make sure that the poor head did not remain on the ground. The younger boy felt offensively light, inconsequential. Aidan gulped back the angry tears that sprang into his throat. While he carried his friend into the novices' hut, he murmured Psalm Forty-six. He thought Rory would want it, and he needed to drown out the chanting and noise that escaped from the chapel. He laid the corpse on his own pallet, finished the psalm, and left without crossing himself. He wouldn't lay others to rest—there were simply too many—but he could at least tend to that one.

Aidan was outside the front gate before another coherent thought formed in his mind. He stood motionless under the distant, ice-flecked sky. He had focused all afternoon on getting back to the abbey. Now he had no idea what to do next.

He considered a return to the woods. The thought of Lana, perhaps frightened but safely removed from this horror, made him aware of his own heart still warm in his chest. A measure of strength flowed from there back into his limbs. He longed for the light of her smile, but before he would deserve it he needed to learn if anywhere else could offer more shelter than where she was now—or if others he cared for had found any.

With a swift decision, he ran toward the riverbank. The monks had not mentioned whither the Norsemen had departed, if even they knew. Aidan didn't much care. He could skulk along the banks of the river nearly to his father's land and cottage. Not even the frogs would likely notice him. With luck, he might find some of his family alive—or at least take hope from a home and yard that were empty instead of littered with corpses.

Aidan ran as best he could through the mud and undergrowth fringing the river. When he tripped and sprawled over an obstacle in the reeds, he leapt back up with a cry, afraid he'd stumbled over the dead. It took a moment for his strained senses and throbbing shin to inform him differently. He'd tripped on something hard, something humming numbers he associated with wood, not any silent corpse. Careful probing revealed an oar. It led to a boat. No fisherman's coracle, this; with a chill

Aidan realized he'd stumbled over one of the raiders' craft. That meant they still reveled somewhere nearby, probably waiting for daylight before they would leave.

His heart in his throat and his ears primed for the noise of approach, he eased among the reeds, identifying two small longboats there. Trampled reeds and a track in the mud suggested a third had already departed. Not the dreaded dragon boats of which he'd heard tales, these were each big enough for only ten or twelve men. A great ship probably awaited downriver while small raiding parties like this one pillaged up and down the banks on both sides.

As Aidan fidgeted near the two craft, debating how to use the discovery, he found something else. The river lapped at a pile of manuscript pages, pale under the moon. The silver and bronze hinges that had bound them had been hacked off, the jeweled or gold-foiled covers shorn away. With a cry of dismay, he scrabbled through the soaked sheets and lifted them, dripping. It was too dark to tell which books they had been or even how many lay mutilated there. He only knew they were ruined, defiled for the value of their bindings and decorative trim.

Letting the river take the pages once more, Aidan stood trembling beneath the pricking stars. Fury sparked a vengeful idea. The sooner the raiders moved on, the less damage and death the village would sustain, but he couldn't force his feet away from the boats without striking back.

Prayers for guidance firmed his intent without making him feel it had holy approval. Aidan's conscience whispered that he would be promoting neither Christian forbearance nor peace. He ignored it, making a decision he knew he might pay for with blood. Sweat trickling off his skin despite the cool night air, he tugged and dragged at the narrow ends of the nearest boat until it finally slid into the slime, where the river began lifting its weight.

When it became clear his plan could succeed, Aidan stripped his robe and soft undergarment over his head and tossed them high up the bank. Though his ancestors had routinely gone warring dressed in little but startling blue paint, he was merely being practical: Wet, the clothing would weight and constrain him too much. Neither weapons nor comrades nor battle-lust nor even fierce paint protected him in its stead, though. Feeling deathly vulnerable in the nude, he waded out with the boat until the cold, muddy water rose to his waist. There he rolled over the near gunwale and thumped down inside, letting the lazy current carry the craft into depth.

The river swished eagerly over the same gunwale when he rocked it under and kept it there with his weight. Too seaworthy to go down without struggle, the strange craft bucked and fought him, but Aidan persisted. As the swamping hull slid away beneath him at last, he let himself flow out on the water flowing in. Shivering, he hung on to the failing boat only long enough to be sure it was not simply rolling, but sinking. Then he struck back toward shore, swimming poorly in an effort not to splash.

By the time he reached land, he had a lengthy walk back and nerve-splitting trouble finding the second boat again in the dark among the featureless reed beds. He told himself more than once that discovery meant death, regardless of whether he was found naked or dressed. Still, it took all his will to keep casting through the sharp and rattling reeds rather than searching higher on the bank for his tunic and robe. He listened for the numbers of wood and grunted in both pain and relief when he finally banged his toes on the remaining longboat.

By the time he pulled his clothing back over his head, well over an hour had passed, midnight approached, and the Norsemen would have to retreat from their plunder on foot. With his sabotage done, Aidan began shaking so hard from ignored fear and chill that he could barely get his arms in the sleeves, let alone tie his belt. Somehow, the novice's robe did not seem to fit him as well as it had before. He ran blindly away from the riverside and dropped into the lee of a drystone wall to regain control of himself.

Long minutes of silent shivering slowed his heart from wild panic to mere racing. Trying to rub warmth into himself, Aidan's hands discovered Lana's charm, wet but still secure around his neck. The oak leaves had long ago fallen away, forgotten. He pressed the twiggy cross against his chest, glad he hadn't lost it. The awkward confusion he had felt when she'd slipped it over his neck returned to him, somehow comforting compared to what he'd felt since. He wondered what she was doing at that moment, like him, alone in the dark. Praying, Aidan asked that only boredom and sleepiness might find her. He fingered her charm and hoped that his perhaps foolhardy risk hadn't drained it completely of any protective power it had. He surely still needed it.

Aidan got back to his feet and set out again for home more stealthily than before, knowing he was probably between the invaders and a place they expected to return to. A vengeful twist in his heart made him long to stay there in hiding and watch for their return simply to enjoy their surprise and anger, but he might as well drown himself and die more easily. The dread havoc they'd already wreaked would probably not match their fury when they found they'd taken a loss of their own. By then, any men willing to fight had better be ready and close at hand. That meant that Aidan needed to alert somebody and perhaps join in a battle before he could even think of returning for Lana. Nowhere else would truly be safe until the raiders were departed or dead.

Picturing her curled in her woodsy nook, he felt his heart flop. He had just doubled or tripled the odds that she would remain in hiding alone and be forced to come out on her own a day or two hence. He hoped he hadn't just made a terrible mistake. Any lingering remorse for their kiss vanished.

Curling away from the river at last, Aidan approached a cluster of wicker-and-mud cottages that included his father's. Thatching still smoldered. Other roofless walls gaped up at the sky. The moon, having cast off the clouds, now provided too much cruel light. Doors hung open and farming tools lay where they'd dropped. The eerie hush over every home and hovel strained Aidan's faith even though he knew any survivors would be huddling, cold and motionless, to escape notice.

Then came the corpses. Biting his lip, Aidan stopped and crouched at each shadow only long enough to grasp the outline of faces, when they weren't too battered to be recognizable. He knew them all, but he kept the moans in his throat until he recognized his nearest brother, Gabriel.

"Aw, Gabe." He squeezed his eyes tight so as not to keep seeing the rent in Gabriel's skull. He tottered there next to the body, his hand on his brother's cold and motionless chest, trying to drag enough air into his own chest to ward off the dizziness that suddenly swirled in his head. Gabriel had taught Aidan to swim and skip stones. The peacemaker in a tangle of brothers, he had only just taken a wife, a raven-haired giggler named Sarah, whom Aidan had once thrown an eel at.

"God take your soul, brother," he murmured, rising unsteadily and moving on without looking down again. He didn't have time or safety for grief.

Aidan slid into a tight, icy haze. Though they couldn't be sounding more than a puff in the dust, his footsteps echoed in his head. He zigzagged between slumped forms like an unhurried dog sniffing cold tracks. His eldest brother's wife and young son were just more empty, moonlit faces.

When he finally arrived past the scattered guard of the dead, he stood motionless before the cottage door, stymied. Ajar on darkness, it left him uncertain whether to knock or call a greeting or push silently inside to learn by feel if any kin awaited there. He considered turning away, no longer wanting to know the full sum of the loss.

"Aidan?"

Aidan leapt and whirled, banging the back of his head against the door frame. That call, barely a whisper, seemed surely to have come from somebody dead.

A shadow darted around the corner of the cottage and threw arms around him. Aidan flailed in an instant of panic before he realized the shadow was solid and warm and emitting a quiet sound of nine that he recognized.

"I saw you approach," the shadow whispered, holding firm. "I just didn't know it was you. And then I feared you must be a wraith."

"Liam!" Aidan embraced his oldest brother and buried his face in a work-hardened shoulder. As tall as Liam, he still felt like a small, clinging boy. He didn't care.

"Praise God you were spared," Liam murmured. "The heathens already sent a boatload of captives downriver. I'm told many were monks. Things must have gone hard at the abbey."

"Like here, from the looks." Aidan drew back to peer at his brother's eyes in the darkness, seeing mostly a dead wife and child instead. He crushed a fold of Liam's tunic in one fist.

"Your . . . yours have found peace, Liam," he said. "Trust it."

Liam flinched, looking away. After swallowing twice, he managed, "I came back to make sure of it. I won't leave them all night for the crows."

"Who else?" Aidan reached his hand to the door.

"No." Liam stopped him. "Don't go in."

"Who?"

Groaning, Liam cupped one hand around the back of Aidan's neck and dropped his forehead to meet Aidan's own.

"Both Mother and Father. Gabriel. He traded his life for Sarah's, and more bitter the draft that I could not do the same. I was too far away. They took Regan prisoner, but she may be dead by now, too. I'd almost rather. Plus . . . the two you already seem to know." He drew a ragged breath. "I am glad to take you off the accursed list."

The names and faces seeped into Aidan one at time and then all at once, like a douse of cold water atop a trickle. There were only Liam and Michael left. His knees wavered. Liam braced him until he got his legs straight again.

Aidan's mouth worked, trying to find words for questions he didn't really want answered. He finally settled on just one.

"Quick, most of them? Or hard?" He couldn't quite keep the sob from his whisper.

Liam exhaled at length. "Think about who I've just named. Mostly hard, that I saw. Fighting."

Aidan closed his eyes to focus on breathing. His lungs seemed to be working only in gasps. He raised his eyelids again right away, disturbed by the pictures his mind tried to invent.

"Well, there's going to be more fighting to do," he

growled. "I've just sunk the rest of their boats. They won't leave at dawn, or if they do, they won't be hard to follow. Where are Michael, and Gabe's wife, and—"

"Lying low in the smithy. What are you talking about?"

With savage satisfaction, Aidan told him.

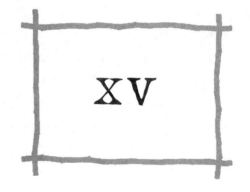

XV

Aidan helped his brother bear their dead kin to the cottage. Liam still would not let him in past the doorway, and Aidan decided to trust his brother's conviction that he would not want to know the carnage done to those already shrouded in shadows. Closer views of the bodies outside as they lifted and carried them were painful enough.

With that task done quickly, he followed Liam to the smithy. What was left of the clan, perhaps twoscore souls, took shelter there among the half-finished tools and hot coals that could serve as protection, if needed. Lamplight joined the ruddy glow of the forge, however, and the tension had dropped since Liam had left them. Another man had returned from a similar mission to report that the Norsemen were encamped at the brewster's home. Aidan knew the place, which always smelled of roast pork and served as an alehouse for those pilgrims with silver to trade for beer and a bite. A score of Vikings crammed into it now, drinking heartily, as cheerful and tamed as pilgrims themselves—because they had taken possession of Donagh's only legitimate son and the most likely heir to his reign.

Aidan remembered the hooded figure whisked through the woods by the raiders. His stomach cramped. The village sat in the eye of a storm, then, not near its end. The raiders had given Donagh until morning to consider his love for his son and gather a ransom more enticing than the price of a slave. The jovial and cooperative mood perhaps explained why they had left no one guarding their boats. It also explained why no force of Donagh's guards, however bloodied and ragtag, had come to the defense of the people or to rally the men. Instead, the lord's most trusted comrades were probably riding hard to his allies to offer land or cattle for silver. A highborn hostage had engendered a temporary truce.

If the Norsemen discovered their loss before getting their ransom, however, they might prefer vengeance to trade. The young lordling's death would fall on Aidan's head, followed eventually by Donagh's wrath. If the ransom and hostage changed hands before the secret came out, the raiders would keep their prize and the fighting would burst open again anyway. They weren't likely to stroll away down the riverbank, overladen with booty, without drawing more blood first.

"Fool!" shrieked old Muirne Connach, rising to slap at Aidan when the latest news had been told. "The deaths of any left here fall on you! Should have been you carted downriver to slavery instead of my Sean!"

The old woman's feeble blows hurt Aidan less than her loathing, but one of her relatives quickly corralled her. As others watched with pained sympathy, the fellow pulled her aside to say, "He didn't know. If no noble had been taken for ransom, blood still may have been flowing tonight. We would be planning a riverside ambush, and you'd be calling him hero instead."

"Fie!" spat Muirne. "Call a curse upon him, that is what I should do!"

The onlookers blanched.

"Not under my roof, you won't." The metalsmith stepped up, alarmed, as if his roof and not Aidan had been threatened with evil. "It might miss its mark."

"Not to mention he does not deserve it," Liam growled.

"He's one of us, Grandmother, not one of them." The younger Connach drew the distraught elder back to her remaining family. "And you're a fierce old woman, but no conjuring crone, so stop pretending. I know you're aggrieved, we all are, but not by Aidan O'Kirin. Let him be."

Liam and the other men discussed the dilemma in weary voices. Aidan only listened, his head low. He could not regret taking a tiny bite at the Norsemen in exchange for the deaths of people he loved, but clearly his action had made matters worse.

The men decided to send a messenger to alert Donagh that the bargain would be more complicated than it seemed. It was the ruler's right and responsibility, after all, to make decisions and lead the defense. Aidan offered to run the bad news up the hill to the lord's ring fort. Liam would have none of it.

"You're not a good liar, Aidan," he said. "If he asks who sank the boats, you'll either tell him outright or he will know from your face. He may run you through on the spot."

"Better my blood than another's," Aidan whispered, his mouth dry. He stuffed his hands into the cuffs of his sleeves to cover their trembling, which he did not want Liam to see. " 'Tis my fault. I'll take the blame."

"No. I intend to protect you better than that. I have few enough others left."

Instead, Aidan's childhood friend Kyle would go, claiming ignorance of the culprit's identity. As he prepared to leave, Aidan embraced him. A rush of memories flowed through him, wafted by the tingling three that had always been Kyle's number.

"Forgive me your errand," Aidan said. "I would walk out with you, knock you on the head, and go in your place, but you know Liam. He'll hang on to my sleeve until you're long up the hill."

"And your brother is right," Kyle said. "But what makes you think I would fall to a blow delivered by you?"

They both grinned about old times, and Kyle clapped Aidan's back.

" 'Tis good to see you," he added. "I wish it were over a mutton shank instead. Are they letting you out of the abbey walls now, or are you free only because of the raid?"

Aidan dropped his eyes. "I'm not supposed to be out." He didn't know what else to say. He wasn't sure if brothers Eamon and Nathan would allow him back in. He had no idea whether he wanted them to.

"Aidan, defying a rule?" Kyle snorted. "Monkhood has indeed changed you, my friend, but not as I might have expected."

Aidan studied the wry grin on his friend's tired and somehow aged face, wondering how he'd slipped from last week's humble obedience to this tumult of impulse and confusion. It wasn't so much the Viking attack, he decided, as a certain young woman who would not admit to being a witch.

"I have found a few things at the abbey that I did not expect, either," he said.

Just then, as Aidan had predicted, Liam approached to stay within arm's length of him.

"Indeed?" Kyle said. "Well, perhaps you can tell me more later." He gently slapped Aidan's cheek, a taunt long swapped between them. Aidan expected a jibe to follow, as when they were younger. After a moment of hesitation, however, Kyle just shook his head and said, "Until I see you again."

"Godspeed," Aidan murmured. He watched his friend, looking oddly too large, disappear into the night. It made him feel both guilty and strangely calm, as if they'd both grown so much older that whatever happened next didn't matter.

Behind him, Liam drummed a fist on his shoulder. "Depending on what Donagh chooses to do, we will likely still need men to lift weapons—but there may not be much work for a monk. Should you get back to the monastery?"

"I'm going to fight with you until this is done."

"I cannot imagine your brothers in God will approve." Liam tipped his head, studying Aidan. "Don't turn your back on what you want, not over one mistake."

Aidan lowered his chin to rub the nape of his neck, partly in uncertainty and partly because he wanted to escape that knowing gaze. He mumbled, "I don't know what I want anymore, Li."

"Then this is not the time to decide. There's too much blood on the grass for good decisions anytime soon. Go back, Aidan. We can handle what comes without you."

Liam's face, however, showed the doubt Aidan felt.

Perhaps aware that he had not been convincing, Liam added softly, "And I'd like to know that at least one O'Kirin will survive till next week."

Aidan tried to picture himself walking back to the abbey and dropping to his knees there. Now that his initial horror had grown cold, his repugnance and anger overlaid with even more blood and loss, he could better understand and perhaps even forgive the numb acceptance with which the senior monks had faced calamity. Without magnificent books in the library, however, it was harder to envision a place for himself among them.

There was somewhere else, though, that he longed to return to.

"Do you think Donagh will do anything before morning?" he asked.

"If I were him, I'd attack now. They are all in one place, unsuspecting, and probably drunk."

"But his heir—" Aidan protested.

"Yes. He would have to forfeit his son, and I doubt he's man enough to do that. His idiot son's life is worth ten or twenty of ours."

"Idiot?"

"He's older than you, Aidan, with a horse and arms and the training to use them. Would you have allowed yourself to be captured alive, knowing how many would suffer to recoup a ransom?"

Aidan grimaced. Liam had a point. After pacifying the Vikings with silver and gold, Donagh's attention would turn to rebuilding his wealth. He'd mount raids of his own on distant enemies, with local men bound to take part. In their absence, the crops left unburned by the Vikings would languish. The late autumn would echo with danger and blood, and the coming winter might be brittle with hunger.

"I would not have been taken alive for a ransom of stones," Aidan said. He was not sure it was true, but he hoped the truth would reflect in Liam's reaction. Outside the abbey for the first time in long months, he needed help in remembering who he was when no monkish expectations confined him.

"Exactly," said Liam, with gratifying certainty. He added, "But go be a monk. Pray for the rest of us. That may help more than a scythe blade in your hands."

Aidan gnawed his lip. "I can pray here. At least until Kyle returns with some word." Faltering, he added, "If there's night left before whatever will come, I might leave for a time. I'll be back, though."

"You don't mean the abbey, from the looks of you." When Aidan only flinched and kept his eyes low, Liam pressed, "Aidan, if I didn't know better I would think you were trysting."

Willing the blush back out of his face, Aidan said, "When the attack started, I ended up with a . . . a prisoner of the abbey. Who's now hiding in the woods. I just want to check that she's still all right."

"She, is it? I was right, then." A wry chuckle broke through Liam's weariness. "Oh, you are in turmoil, aren't you, little brother? But she'll be safer in the woods awhile yet."

"I want to make sure," Aidan said, trying to ignore Liam's teasing.

Nodding, Liam let it rest there. Aidan found a quiet corner and took the suggestion to pray. He split the time evenly between pleading with God to protect his remaining family and friends and searching his heart for an impossible path between monkhood and a girl waiting near an uprooted tree.

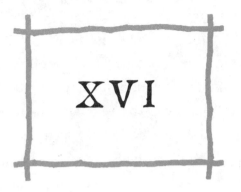

XVI

Kyle returned in less than an hour on the back of a horse reined by one of Donagh's stable boys. The refugees gathered around for news.

They were given only the instruction to hold cover until after dawn. The lord stuck to the planned payment of ransom and had decided he would also offer horses and wagons to speed the Norsemen's departure. He was betting they would not learn about their boats before then.

After the stable boy left, the men sat around the forge, grumbling.

"At least he's trying to stem the bloodshed," muttered Liam. "Though from cowardice, I suspect, not compassion."

"He's doing nothing to prepare for the worst, either," complained Michael, Aidan's middle brother. "Not protecting his people tonight, in case the Vikings discover their craft gone, nor ransoming any other captives, so far as we know."

"Regan might be hauled off in one of those carts!" Aidan realized, the notion pricking new outrage from him. He'd begun to think of his sister as already dead.

"And my two sons," agreed the cartwright, "if their hearts are still beating. Borne away in a cart that I built—an evil sight that will be. If I had no wife and old mother to feed, I would make sure yon Norsemen closed my eyes with a blade before I saw that."

"Liam," Aidan said, "I like your idea better." He hesitated. "Why can't we hit them ourselves? With the same method they use—set the alehouse afire and kill the vermin one at a time as they flee it."

"This is the monk talking?" Kyle asked.

Aidan ignored him. The tumult in his heart left no room just now for questions of faith, humility, or obedience.

"But there is a truce on while Donagh's collecting their ransom," the smith's apprentice protested. " 'Tis not honorable warfare to break it."

"They're Vikings, not a nobleman's forces," somebody snapped.

Liam added darkly, "Honorable men do not slay four-year-old boys."

"Lord Donagh would have our heads, though," sighed Michael. "We might as well sever and stake them ourselves."

His objection drew murmurs of agreement.

"Too bad Widow Connach cannot truly fling curses," mused Kyle. "We could use such arts right now."

"Bite your tongue," the smith said. "Weird-women have ears in the trees. One may bend her cunning to our sorrow instead of our gain."

The words sparked inspiration in Aidan. While the others stared glumly into the fire, his mind raced. A grim smile pulled at his lips.

"Donagh won't care what we do," he said, "as long as his son isn't killed. We just have to keep him alive when we do it."

"And how would you propose we accomplish that?" Michael demanded, his frustration showing. "As if you had battle experience, Aidan. Try harder to not be a fool." He and Aidan had always sparked against each other, and the day's strain added fuel.

Aidan licked his lips. Most of the men, aware Michael was older, did not look for Aidan to answer. Yet enough hope mixed with the doubt on their faces to encourage him.

He said, "If someone walked into the alehouse just before the fire was set and could locate Brendan Donagh, possibly that person could protect him until the smoke was thick enough to cover."

"Slitting his throat is the first thing they'll do," Michael retorted.

"Maybe not," Aidan countered calmly. "Not if they think the person walking in is a witch."

His comrades erupted with uneasy laughter and protests. The women and children huddling in the corners looked over, concerned.

"You've all gone daft," the smith grumbled.

"Kyle suggested a curse," Aidan continued over the furor. "A conjurer in the flesh would be far more disarming."

Peppered with questions, he paid attention only to Liam, who now headed the family and whom Aidan respected most. His eldest brother simply wanted to know where Aidan expected to find a witch willing to help them.

"Never mind where," Aidan said. "But I—"

"Oh, I'm sure the monastery is full of the Devil's assistants," Michael said, rolling his eyes.

"Be silent, Michael." Liam's sharp voice cut off Michael's sneer.

Ignoring the interruption, Aidan went on, "I can find out how to pass for a witch myself, for a few moments—just enough to surprise them and get close to the lord's heir. After that it won't matter."

"Have you taken leave of your senses?" Liam wondered. "The glare of a witch would likely freeze their entrails, I admit. Mine too, come to that, if I didn't know it for a ruse. Yet soon enough they would thaw. Young Donagh's throat might be cut first, but yours would soon follow."

Aidan regarded him coolly, almost forgetting the others around them. "I am not so docile as that, Liam. I won't be bound. If I have any weapon at all, I can defend myself for a moment. If I can, I'll loose him to defend himself. They won't fight for long once the rafters are burning."

"I will vouch for Aidan's skill with makeshift weapons," Kyle said softly, "if he can fight as well in earnest as he used to face me in jest."

"He should," said a neighbor. "He is obviously mad."

"And you're being sheep!" Aidan clutched at the dark streaks on his robe. "Have you forgotten the blood we're all wearing? And who it belonged to?"

Liam put his hand on Aidan to calm him.

"Enya and Kevin," Aidan hissed at him, flinging the names of the dead like sharp stones. "Would you bear their slaughter with only a shrug?" He half expected his brother to hit him, and he knew he deserved it, but he also knew it took drastic words to provoke someone who hummed of nine.

Liam only closed his eyes, the muscles in his jaw twitching. Nobody said anything for several uncomfortable moments. Eyes shifted their gaze from one person to the next. Aidan could see the men consider his suggestion, and he knew they would follow Liam.

"It would be suicide, likely," the eldest O'Kirin said finally. He opened his eyes and drilled them into Aidan.

"Martyrdom, if you like, although not strictly for God. Is it worth that, Aidan?"

If Liam's voice had held even a hint of condescension, Aidan might have fallen on habit and bowed to the judgment of his eldest brother. The respect in Liam's eyes, though, gave Aidan pause. He knew what Liam's answer to that question would be, but Liam would yield. Aidan had to answer this one for himself.

He imagined dying under a quick, heavy stroke from a hulking Viking. Then he thought about the blow that felled Rory and the torn flesh of his own family members. If they could all die as they had, without choice, then he could die to avenge them.

"If those of you waiting outside do your part well enough," he said softly, "then, yes."

"And this is how you would have me protect you?" Liam wondered, mostly to himself.

"Think what our family name stands for, Li, and why O'Kirins have fought in the past," Aidan urged. "I would rather you bury valor than protect cowardice."

"Numb-witted valor, in that case," Michael argued. "If you fail, you're not the only one who will die. We may kill all the Norsemen tonight, only to follow them ourselves on the morrow as traitors. Donagh's fury will rage."

"Are you so afraid of meeting God and your namesake, Michael?" Aidan asked. "But Lord Donagh will not be there to watch. Work fast and get back here. If I can escape with his accursed son, he won't care. If I fail, who will give him your names? The brewster? Not likely. I can't imagine he and his wife are enjoying their guests. All Donagh will see when he arrives at sunup is a yard full of dead Vikings. My body can bear all the blame. He can't hang our whole clan—not with so few left—and he won't know where else to start."

"It is tempting," Kyle murmured.

"It is more than tempting," Liam said. "Except I don't know why they would believe you're a witch."

"Let me worry about that," Aidan said. "That's the simplest part."

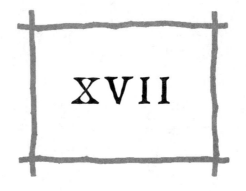

XVII

Without hours hidden by sleep, the night stretched impressively long. As he hurried back toward the woods, Aidan felt grateful for all the time he could get. He'd spoken bravely enough, and he meant it, but he wasn't sure he would live to see dawn.

Guilt, as well as dread, burdened his belly. The Gospels spoke of forgiveness and peace. Kyle had been justified in wondering that a monk—even a wavering one—would urge violence. Yet Aidan had also been told of armed monks storming rival abbeys over relics and wealth. Surely if one monk could raise a weapon against another without being damned, then Aidan could, with a clear heart, bring righteous war to invaders. He clung to that hope. God's judgment of his choice would be delivered all too soon.

Once he was well into the trees, another worry began

to simmer in Aidan's chest. Knowing the Norsemen to be relaxed in truce, he'd left the smithy with a lit tallow lamp so he wouldn't flounder so much finding his way. The light did not help him enough. He knew roughly where Lana's shelter must lie, but he had paid too little attention arriving the first time, when he'd simply followed her. Now he wasn't sure he could find it again.

After more stumbling and casting about than he would have admitted, he finally gave up on his eyes. Instead he tried reaching with some other sense. It couldn't have worked with anyone else; so many people buzzed of the same numbers, at any distance their sounds merged to surround him in noise as meaningless as silence. But Aidan heard eleven only from Lana. Any eleven-ish hum he caught now would have to be her. He'd never met a cat in the woods.

His lashes veiled his eyes. Peeping out just enough to avoid walking headlong into trees, Aidan slowed and trolled the forest for her hum. He might have been imagining it, but he thought he recognized her sound a little farther east than his feet had been aiming. He turned that way.

Once he stopped looking for the uprooted tree, he came across it almost immediately. The shadow of the leaning trunk jumped out at him, and he recognized the root wall at its end.

"Lana," he called, to prevent startling her. Aidan shoved through the hawthorn gate, ignoring the thorns grasping at him. He froze.

The hollow was empty. No eleven hummed there, and no Lana awaited; the lamp left no doubt. The ground where Aidan had drawn Latin letters had been brushed smooth. The only evidence that either of them had been there was the scent of recently trampled fern fronds.

Aidan burst back outside, calling loudly. A thorn ripped at his neck and he fought briefly to break the hawthorn's grip on his robe.

"Lana!" he repeated. "Where are you?"

He stopped calling abruptly. If she'd been within earshot and able, she would have answered already. Perhaps she'd given in to the longing for news of her mother. Aidan knew roughly where her mother's cottage must lie, but not surely enough to find it in the dark.

The flickering lamp cast threatening shadows in the branches and brush around him. He closed his eyes to shut them out and took a deep breath, trying to decide what to do.

As his thoughts slowed, he again caught the far-off

purr of Lana's eleven. Alarm had risen to drown it when he had realized she wasn't where he'd expected. Now he turned in place, trying to fix it. He should have realized at once that she could not be here; that hum was too faint. He walked farther east, slowly, covering the ground with as little attention to his body as he could manage, because thinking of low branches and sharp rocks and brambles made the humming harder to hear. He followed the soft sound like the distant shush of falling water.

He found her shadow crouched alongside the creek a stag's flight or more from the uprooted tree.

"Lana?"

She squeaked, startled, before she whirled and recognized his face in the lamp's glow. He heard her splash something into the water before rising to meet him. After an awkward instant, they embraced.

"You worried me," he said. "Why did you leave your shelter?"

"I couldn't stay there without even a candle," she said. "Once the light was all gone, I heard too many frightening things in the blackness. I felt trapped. And I didn't expect you to come back. At least not so soon."

"I told you I would."

"I'm sorry. I'm not used to someone who does what he

says," she murmured. "Most people don't. I thought you'd just stay at your abbey. Is everyone safe there?"

He looked away into the darkness. "No." Not ready to relive those scenes yet, he changed the subject. "What were you doing just now? In the water?" He had spotted the wooden bowl in her hand and recognized it as the one from her nook. She may have been merely getting a drink, but Aidan didn't think so. Even when he had been able to see no more than her shadowy shape against the gleam of the creek, something about her position had alerted him that she'd been unusually intent on the bowl.

Lana lowered the bowl to the farthest extent of her arms and wrapped both hands around it as if she would just as soon stash it behind her back. "Oh . . . do you want to go back to my hiding place? 'Twill be cozy enough with the lamp."

Her clumsy dodge of his question sharpened his interest. When she started to step away, he didn't move.

She took only a few steps. When she saw he wasn't following, she stopped at the outer reach of the lamplight. Standing motionless and silent for several long breaths, she finally whispered, "I'm afraid to tell you."

"Why?"

"You might . . . be scared of me. Or hate me."

Apprehension built in his belly, but he couldn't guess what she might mean.

She took his silence as confirmation of her fears. "Why do things we can't understand have to come from the Devil?" she protested. "Surely we do not understand everything about God."

Aidan gnawed the inside of his cheek, his dread doubling. He resisted the desire to retreat a step. Instead, he pressed, "Tell me, Lana. What have you done?"

"Well . . . I was trying to scry in the moonlight," she said, low. "I needed to see what had become of my mother."

After all her reluctance, and the abundance of gore he'd seen that day, Aidan had begun to imagine some rite with lamb's blood and severed parts of a bird. He exhaled in relief. Then his mind engaged what she had said.

"You can scry?" Catching glimpses of other places or times in a bowl of moonlit water was as likely as seeing a leprechaun—or so Aidan had been taught.

"Sometimes," she said. "With the moon out of round, what I saw might not be true, but I think she's all right."

Her plaintive hope emboldened him—and summoned his guilt. He should have reassured her immediately.

"Your mother is fine, I've been told." He had asked at

the smithy. "The raiders bypassed homes that far down-river to hit the abbey more quickly."

Relief washed over Lana's face in the moonlight. "It's true, then! Oh, thank you!"

The joyous rise in her voice lifted Aidan's heart, too. Now and again Lana made him uneasy, but the rest of the time, she drew him like an ant to honey.

Eyeing her bowl, which she no longer tried to hide, he snorted and shook his head. "I knew you were a witch."

"I'm not bad, though. I would never hurt anyone. I'm just a . . . a wood-witch, I guess. Nothing evil!"

"I didn't say you were. But you do make me nervous."

"You make me nervous," she countered. The idea was so laughable, he didn't bother asking why. He figured she had said it only for argument's sake.

"Then we're even," he said. "But I'm glad you finally admitted it—because I need your help with something." He took two paces to catch up to her. "Shall we return to your tree now? I'd really like to rest."

She nodded and led him straight back to the upthrust gnarl of roots.

They sat down inside and he explained, as briefly as he could, all that had happened to him since he'd left her. When he talked of finding the bodies, his voice dropped. In some trick of memory and talking and time, he abruptly came back from the shadows of his family's cottage to find himself here once more, fallen silent, his head propped in his hands.

Lana reached to stroke his shoulder in sympathy. For a moment, he rested silent in that bittersweet distraction. Then he raised his face and traded his sorrow for the thin consolation of vengeance. Relating the news of the ransom, Aidan described what he and his kinsmen planned instead.

"So can you tell me how to behave like a witch?" he finished. "Something frightening?"

She gazed silently at the knuckles of her clenched hands.

"I don't mean to make fun of you," he added, afraid he had insulted her. "I just thought you would know something to distract them with. You've startled me without even trying."

Still she didn't reply.

"Lana, won't you help me?" Aidan pleaded, gripped with fear that his plan would fall undone on such a small hurdle. He could invent a ploy without her advice, he supposed, but the notion sent a flush of cold terror through him. The thought of walking alone into a house he would probably never walk out of was dreadful enough. He didn't think he could make his feet do it without the confidence of an authentic act.

"No," she said softly.

He dropped his head back into his hands.

"What you're talking about is going to be terribly dangerous, Aidan," she said. "Pretending won't be enough. You'll need real witchery." She looked up. "I'll do it for you."

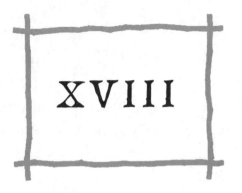

XVIII

When Aidan recovered his tongue, he couldn't spill his protests quickly enough for them to make sense.

"Don't be a fool," he told Lana. "I thought about that, but I can't let a girl—Could you really . . . ? No. No, I won't allow that. I'm going. They might believe you're a witch faster, but . . ." Hearing himself, Aidan stopped to collect his wits.

She folded her arms and watched him, her lips a tight line. Finally he came up with a sound argument. "It won't work," he said firmly. "You'll be useless for rescuing Donagh's heir."

"I have no interest in keeping Brendan Donagh alive," she said flatly. "But I do care about *you* staying alive. We can both go, if you'd rather. In fact, that will make it easier to scare them. If you want to save their hostage, that's your problem."

"But even if it works, Lana . . ." His voice trailed off again as he traced the possibilities to their likely and unlikely conclusions. "As it is, you no longer exist. Nobody at the abbey has even thought about you, and when they do, they'll assume you were captured or killed. Even Donagh will think you are dead. So you can do what you want. But if anyone sees you with me—"

"I won't be any worse off than I was this morning."

"We both very well may be killed," he said, hardly wanting to admit it to himself. "That will be much worse."

A sly and almost sinister smile crept onto her face. "Aidan, you haven't much faith in your witch."

While he tried to decide how much she was joking, she fingered her lips and gazed at him with unfocused eyes. Nodding to herself and rising, she declared, "I'll need branches of holly and yew. Might as well take a sprig of hawthorn, since it is here." She snapped a twig off the bush blocking the entrance and slid its thorny length carefully into a pocket of her mantle. "And elder, perhaps—if I dare. Bring your lamp and help me find them."

He argued with her as she crept through the woods looking for just the right trees. She barely responded, and Aidan felt his resistance wearing away. His shoulders drooped under the weight of her possible death, but now that he'd set her in motion, he wasn't sure how to stop her. Certainly his words were not working.

After the yew had been found, Lana hushed him. She bowed her head before the tree and asked for permission to harm it.

"I ask with full understanding of the results I may reap," she added. "May I proceed?"

Aidan shivered, the tone of her voice banishing the fond idea that she was playing a harmless if childish game. He waited with her, wondering what kind of answer she expected. She gazed into the shadowy branches while the night breeze lifted and sighed through the needles. Then she reached to stroke nearby boughs as though the tree were a prickly pet.

Lana let loose a long sigh of her own. "Thank you," she breathed. Quickly she found a bough of arm's length that she wanted, bent it back, and stripped it from the tree like a handful of feathers plucked from a goose. She passed it to Aidan.

"Don't drop it," she warned, her voice sharp. "Don't lose even a needle, if you can help it. And for your soul's sake, don't let the lamp flame get close."

"I won't," he murmured. The gravity of her voice and her rite made him feel as though he bore a severed limb. Skin crawling, he cradled the bough against his chest.

Lana moved on in search of a holly. He followed in silence.

She startled him from dark thoughts with a cry of recognition. The prickly leaves of a holly bush glinted in the lamplight. She took a long time finding a branch with exactly nine sprigs of leaves. Aidan watched, remembering all the bad-luck tales he'd ever heard about holly. He grew even more uneasy when she called, not quite singing,

> *King Holly, give me of thy bright, white wood,*
> *And I will give thee of my bones*
> *When I am dead and laid to molder*
> *Underneath a tree.*

Fingering her chosen bough, she peered abruptly past Aidan to the sky. "Where's the moon now?" she wanted to know, shading her eyes from the lamp with her free hand.

He caught that hand to halt her. "Lana, stop. Never mind. I won't mind dying so much, if that's what will happen. I think our Father in Heaven will still raise me when the Messiah returns, even if I have been a lousy novice today. But I really do not want your death on my head."

"Why—you think He won't raise me, too?"

"I'm not joking."

"Neither am I." She squeezed his hand. "You thought it was worth doing before, Aidan. If you're right, then 'tis worth doing as best we can do it, so there might be some chance it will work."

She brushed her fingers through the bough trapped in his other arm.

"Besides," she added, "it is already begun."

"We could just go back to the smithy," he said, "and let Donagh pay his ransom."

"You're not listening, Aidan. No, we can't. I've ripped a branch from the Tree of Life and Death with violent intent and on your behalf. It is too late to stop now. The yew will give both of us life or death, one or the other, before we are done, whether we go to the alehouse or not. We might as well go and finish your plan. Our fate will be the same either way."

Aidan's tongue stuck in his mouth. His training told him not to believe what she'd said. He couldn't help it. Her steely gaze pierced the intense waves of eleven that battered his ears, rising from her now like heat off a coal. The sharpening pitch of that number convinced him.

He only bowed his head and nodded.

Lana checked the sky again, the eastern horizon this time. "How long until dawn, do you think?"

"A few hours yet," he said. As they'd begun searching for holly, he'd heard the abbey bell distantly tolling for Matins. So the new day was still many praises and prayers away.

Lana sat down away from the holly, where the leaf litter would not feel so prickly. "We might as well rest a bit, then. I'd rather wait until the moon sets to take a branch of the holly. It'll be stronger that way."

"Stronger for what?"

When she didn't answer, he gave up and settled beside her. He asked her permission to set the yew branch on the ground alongside. She let him lay it down only after removing her mantle to spread beneath it. Aidan felt as though she'd begun to speak a separate language, one he didn't know but whose powerful words would determine the fates of them both.

That uncomfortable notion reminded him of something that seemed to have taken place days ago. "Did you learn the letters I showed you?" he asked.

She nodded, a smile alighting on her face for the first time since they'd departed the uprooted tree. She recited the sounds. With the tip of one finger, she traced the shapes, not on the ground but on his leg, which he'd stretched out alongside her. "*Ah*," she repeated, her finger moving, "*bay . . .*"

The wool of Aidan's robe was thick, but not so thick that her touch didn't send a shiver the length of his body.

Without thinking, he reached to stop her hand, trapping it against his leg before it could tickle *kay* or *dhay*. The abrupt motion startled them both.

Their eyes met—as much as they could in the flickering glow of the lamp. The shadowed hollows hiding Lana's blue eyes drew an unexpected shudder from Aidan, recalling dark splashes of blood masking the true colors of clothing and flagstones and grass.

"There was so much blood, Lana," he murmured, aware that his unprompted words would probably only confuse her. "I can still smell it now. It won't go away."

She looked down at his hand holding hers captive. "I can see it on your robe in the lamplight," she murmured. "And I could see part of what you've seen on your face, when you told me. I'm so sorry."

Slipping her hand from his grasp, she raised it to the hawthorn scratch on his neck and coursed her fingertips down alongside it. Aidan knew she meant it as a comfort, but that's not how his skin wanted to receive it. His own fingers lifted to touch the pale fire of her hair, tangling in it.

She did not pull away. Instead her hand shifted. Her fingertips stroked his cheek from the corner of his eye to his jaw.

"I wish I knew a tree charm that could wipe that sadness

away," she whispered. "Willow catkins, perhaps, or balsam from the buds of an aspen. If this were the spring."

Aidan didn't move a muscle, afraid of quenching the spark between them. Bloody corpses still cluttered his mind, but they'd faded behind the brightness of Lana.

She leaned in, veering sideways, and brushed his cheek with her lips. A sharp intake of breath betrayed him. Her body was much too close for his comfort. When she straightened, however, that movement away felt even worse.

He drew on the hand in her hair, pulling her back. She hid her eyes behind her lashes but came directly to him. He kissed her until he could barely breathe. Naught and None boomed through his head. Aidan had to tip himself back to clear his ears and snatch a breath.

Given fresh air, his sluggish brain whispered that his lips had no business touching hers. "I cannot do this," he murmured, sliding his hand back out of her hair. "I'm supposed to be a monk."

Lana nestled her head to his shoulder. It took a moment for her soft words to reach his ears and add up in his mind.

"Are you sure? You're like no monk I've ever met."

He looked down at her, almost in his lap, his thoughts lining up poorly. They got lost in her whirring eleven and the warm, musky scent of her skin. Her lips, her eyes, the soft swells under her shift blotted out both the blood splashed that night and, behind that, his time in the abbey.

Giving up his soul and his hopes, Aidan kissed her again.

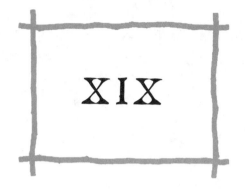

XIX

Aidan explored the feel and taste of Lana's lips, the underside of her jaw, and her throat. His hands began roaming over her shift, tracing the arc of her waist to her lean belly and then back to the maddening mounds of her breasts. The mysterious None of her kisses roared through him, wiping his own identity blank and heaving all other numbers aside.

He wasn't sure why or precisely when her soft yielding changed, but it did. Abruptly, None ebbed. Aidan cringed at the loss. An instant later, Lana stopped pulling him close and instead pushed him back.

"Aidan, wait."

He gazed at her through a fog. With effort, he pulled his awareness back from his body and at least partly into his head so he could understand what she said.

"I'm sorry," she told him, her voice fluttery. "I don't know what you think, but I won't lift my skirts for you.

Even knowing what dawn may bring us. I—I am just not ready to do that."

Aidan gaped, as amazed by her frank words as by the refusal they carried. Then confusion swirled through him.

"What are we doing, then?" he asked, low. Surely she felt at least some of the force that kept knocking him, breathless, to None. He knew she did: Lana's hands had been on him as well.

Her eyes darted from side to side as though she hoped someone else would appear to answer his question.

"Kissing?" Her voice rose uncertainly at the end.

Aidan ran a hand through his hair. His fist clenched in it, pulling, and he exhaled hard. Their exchange had seemed like quite a bit more than just kissing to him. His entire body throbbed.

She tried to smile. "It wouldn't matter, anyway. The hawthorn would stop you if I didn't."

At his bewildered look, she giggled and patted the pocket of the mantle nearby. Aidan remembered, fuzzily, that she'd slipped a hawthorn twig there.

"Doors are not the only things hawthorn will guard," she explained. "Mothers put hawthorn beneath daughters' beds to make sure they remain virgins. 'Tis in my pocket, not under my bed, but . . ." Her wry grin spreading, she raised her palms and dropped them helplessly.

Her gentle humor worked in reverse. A flash of frustration seared through Aidan at her lighthearted tone. He did not catch his tongue before he'd snapped, "I thought your virginity was already stolen."

She recoiled as if she'd been slapped. "That doesn't count," she whispered, turning away and hiding her face in her shoulder.

Aidan felt her wave of hurt and shame like a lash across his chest. Drawing a wobbly breath through that sting, he kneaded one clenched hand with the other, unsure how to regain control of his body, let alone soothe the pain he'd dealt her. After several moments of feeling his heart slow and listening to the misery warbling through her eleven, he reached to touch her shoulder. She jerked from beneath his hand. He gritted his teeth.

"I'm sorry," he told her. "I should never have said that, and I'm behaving like a dog. You're just so . . . you tempt me something fierce."

Lana kept her back to him, hugging herself.

Sighing, he repeated, "I'm sorry. I'll go." He did not want to leave her, and he feared what she'd said about the yew, but he didn't know what else to offer.

When she did not contradict him, he picked himself up to his feet.

"Don't," she pleaded then. "Please." She turned halfway back toward him, though she didn't even try to meet his eyes. The night breeze gusted between them and rested again before she added, "The moon isn't down yet."

Aidan tried to interpret those words against what had just happened between them. Without much sense of success, he ventured, "You still want to help me?"

"Aidan," she replied, sounding anguished, "sometimes I think you are stupid on purpose."

With no good answer to that, he stood looking out at the misshapen eye of the moon. It leered through the trees, sinking almost visibly toward the western horizon. His feet wanted to pace, if not escape altogether, but a wave of weariness rolled through his shoulders and back. He let his legs fold again, sitting carefully more than an arm's length from Lana, with his back mostly to her.

After a long time filled only with the murmur of trees, she asked, "How could you say such a thing? I know I made you angry, but . . . still."

"Not angry," he sighed, heartily wishing he'd listened to Michael and sat now by the forge. "Just . . ." He hunted for the right words. Those that came to mind first weren't any he wanted to say to a girl. "Just confused. But you have every right to be angry with me."

"Not angry," she echoed. "Just hurt."

He told her again he was sorry. Afraid more words would make matters worse, but unable to bear the painful chasm between them much longer, Aidan bit his lip and added, "I really did not mean to say that someone else's offense gave me any right to—"

"Stop! I did not share that with you so I could be reminded of it!"

Chastised, he only nodded. He wondered, though, why she had shared it at all.

Lana added, "I so hoped you would be different."

He winced. Then a scab of resentment formed over the sting. After considering and rejecting a great many replies, he gave up and accepted the punishing silence.

She broke it herself. "No, I take that back, Aidan. That was unfair."

He had been thinking the same thing, but the regret in her voice drew out his own once again. He replied, "What I said before wasn't fair, either. I would take it back if I could."

She did not respond with words, but Aidan could hear her subdued eleven gradually lift to a more ethereal tone. His heart wanted to follow that rise and bask once more in her favor, so he took a deep breath and a chance.

"I am not sorry to have had you in my arms, though," he added. "My next embrace may come from a shroud."

Lana made a choked sound he could not interpret, and he feared he had erred yet again. Then she spoke.

"Couldn't we . . . couldn't you just hold me and that's all?"

For an instant, Aidan rejoiced: She seemed to have

forgiven him. Then the question itself took firmer shape in his mind. He blew out a breath weighted with equal parts of frustration and despair. He longed to give her the answer she wanted, but he feared it might be a lie.

"I don't know if I can do that, Lana." He made the mistake of looking over his shoulder at her. Just the shape of her form in the gloom and the prospect of feeling her body against his once more sent a tingle along his skin.

A hopeful smile flicked onto her lips, not sure it should stay. "I can slap hands that travel too far."

Glad the wounded creature had slipped back out of sight, he replied gently, "I'm serious. I don't think I can. You are too overwhelming that close. Better if I stay a short distance away." He rubbed his face. "Especially if I expect to ever return to the abbey."

"Do you?" she asked, after a moment.

"I don't know." He laughed humorlessly. "I don't know what I'm worried about. I probably won't get the chance. I suppose if God spares me past dawn, I should take that as a sign of His will."

Lana didn't reply.

As they watched the moon sink, however, she began talking again, almost to herself. "I know how much power I will be holding in my hands when we go to the alehouse," she said, "but I would be lying if I said I knew without doubt I could wield it. Are you afraid to die, Aidan?"

He considered well before answering, the day's images crowding his head. "I am more afraid of a meaningless life. The end can be sudden and rude, and I would rather need God's correction for trying too hard than earn His disdain for squandering His gifts." He hesitated. "Including you. Which is why I wish you would—"

"It would be easier for me to believe in your God," she overrode him, "if Christians could agree on more things. They can't even agree on the tree that Christ's cross was made from. I've asked the priest and at least twenty pilgrims. That's how I got the idea in the first place—to sell pieces, I mean. Nobody seems to know surely. It doesn't say in the Gospels, does it?"

Surprised, Aidan said, "I don't think so."

"Do you know them by heart?" she wondered.

"No. But I have read all four, and heard them spoken aloud many times."

"Some say poplar," she told him, "and that's why the tree shakes so—it trembles when it remembers how it served. Father Niall told me elder wood formed the cross, and elders have been stunted ever since. It is a powerful wood in matters of death, and a fickle one if you don't respect it enough. But I've never met someone who has been to the Holy Land to find out if poplar or elder grows there. I've heard that the weather is hot, not like here, so I'm not sure they would. Does either appear in the Gospels?"

Aidan shook his head, disarmed by the depth of her thoughts on the topic. He'd spent many hours of prayer with the crucifix in his mind and never once wondered where the wood had come from before it became a burden for Christ.

"The only other tree in any Scripture story I've ever heard was an olive," she mused. "I don't even know what an olive tree looks like."

"There's a story about Christ and a fig tree," Aidan told her. "He was hungry but the tree didn't have any figs."

"What's a fig?"

"I don't know. I just know you can eat them."

"Not even the Romans would cut down a fruit tree for a crucifix, though. That would be stupid."

"There are lots of other trees in the books of the Bible, though." At her look of surprise, he continued, "Chestnuts and willows and plenty I've never heard of. But most are just mentioned, or the prophets are really talking about powerful people or times of plenty—not the actual trees."

Lana grumbled, "You would think with all that talk about trees they would have said what kind of wood formed the cross."

"Does it matter?" he said. "I mean—"

"It matters to me," she declared. "The kind of tree mattered in Eden, too, didn't it?"

The smile that had crept to Aidan's lips faded. "In man's fall, you mean? I suppose you are right."

"The Tree of Life said to be there could be the rowan. Or the oak. They're both called that. But the yew is the tree of life *and* of death, so I think that might have been it. And since they live almost forever, the cross could have been cut from the same yew. Because Christ died on it, but he rose again to bring eternal life to God's chosen. Life and death and then life."

"The Tree of Life in the garden is the Tree of Life Everlasting," Aidan said. "Not life and death."

"It is? Life Everlasting?"

"That's why Adam and Eve were not to eat of that tree. Only God can bestow life everlasting."

She frowned. "You know that part of the Bible, too?"

"I've read it. In Latin, though, not Greek or Hebrew."

"Hebrew?"

"From the Jews," he explained. "Most of the oldest books were first put down in Hebrew."

Her face fell. "Learning to read Latin won't do me much good then, will it? I never thought of that."

" 'Tis God's Word, whatever the language," he ventured.

"But details change or get lost between one teller and the next." She sighed. "Maybe you could read the tree bits to me sometime, anyhow."

Aidan tried to keep his thoughts off his face. Given their plans and the now barren abbey, reading to her seemed even less likely than teaching her to read for herself. He meant it, though, when he said simply, "I'd like that."

She smiled, but her words revealed the unease in her heart. "If we do not stand before the Tree of Life Everlasting itself before then."

Resisting the desire to spew false reassurance, he said, "Heaven will decide."

She gazed into the sky. "Heaven and the powers of earth," she replied. "The moon has gone down. We'd better get the holly and go."

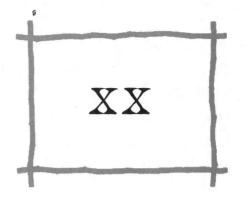

XX

The holly branch Lana had chosen was large enough that she had trouble breaking it off. Having already warned him to silence during the taking, she gestured at Aidan for help. Stepping alongside, he put his hands in place of hers, then twisted and ripped until the shrub let the branch go.

Lana grimaced at the struggle. When the branch finally came loose, she reached over Aidan's head to remove her rowan charm from his neck, hanging it instead on the torn, white stump of the branch. Collecting the yew bough and her mantle as well as the lamp, the pair set off in silence back toward the smithy.

Once out of sight of the holly, Lana spoke. "We can talk again now. The holly did not much want to help us. I hope I haven't made a mistake."

Aidan tried not to feel the lump that formed in his throat at her words. Instead he scanned the eastern horizon for hints of dawn. Though he saw none as yet, he said, "We

should hurry. I don't want them to think I'm not coming."
His mind clung to that small, comfortable fear rather than
face a much greater dread.

With the moon down, speed proved a challenge, and
they both tripped more than once. After they'd emerged
from the woods, the way became easier. Aidan and Lana
worked out a rough plan on their way across the fields.
She would do no more than hint at what she intended to
work with her boughs. She listened carefully, though,
when he recalled what he could, from some years ago,
about the placement of the alehouse door and the furnish-
ings around its central hearth. She had been inside, too,
but now the details could be important to them both.

" 'Tis not that big, not for what might be a score of
men," he said. "We may be within reach of their weapons
right from the doorway." He glanced at her beside him.
With her form overlaid by the images in his mind, his nearest arm rose involuntarily to shield her. It was all he could
do to push it back down, rather than curling it around her
and drawing her far away from raiders and cold blades and
blood.

"Aidan," she said, unaware of his struggle, "once we're
inside, will you be able to hear which of them is their
leader? They must have one, wouldn't you think?"

Afraid of the path her questions were taking, he hedged,
"I don't think they speak Latin."

"That's not what I meant." She cast him a sharp look. "I mean your numbers."

Reluctance, invisible but heavy, dragged at his feet. He struggled to keep trudging through the meadow grass.

"Do all powerful men hum the same?" Lana continued, when he did not respond. "What I do will work best if I can deliver it to the one in charge. 'Enthrall the trunk to enthrall the branches,' so they say."

"Strike the head and Goliath falls," he murmured. She had a point. Unfortunately, it stabbed straight at him.

"Can you?" she pressed.

The easier answer, and the one that would leave him less culpable—*no*—perched on his lips. Holding it back, he searched his mind and his heart for the truth. Given enough time to observe them, he thought he could probably pick out the Viking leader simply by watching. He would not, however, have much time at all for using his eyes.

His sense of numbers flowed immediately, when he was paying attention, but nothing had ever depended on it. Recalling the wounded man at the beekeeper's cottage, he worried that all Norsemen might hum of three. Even if a few sounded of the same fives and sevens and eights common in the dominant men Aidan knew, that knowledge might not be enough. The volume and power and harmonics of any one hum revealed a lot. Those details also took focus and calm to be heard. The pressure to catch and interpret individual sounds in a chaos of strange people and danger daunted Aidan completely.

"I'm not sure," he murmured finally. "I might be able to make a pretty good guess. But it would not be certain, and even if it were, I wouldn't want to count on that, Lana."

Feeling her eyes gauging him, he expected her to encourage or cajole him. He could have more easily discounted either than the response she gave.

"You are counting on my skills," she said quietly. "I will be counting on yours."

Appalled, he shook his head. "I don't want to risk it." He didn't add that it was mostly her life he felt he was risking. He already rued drawing her into such danger. If he made a mistake that directly led to her slaughter, the only comfort would be his own death, and the sooner the better.

"We'll be risking more," she countered, "if you can't help me with that. Find some way to point him out to me. Quickly."

His windpipe tightened around the air trying to flow through it. It cut off the breath he needed to argue. Only the unwavering will in the sound of eleven beside him kept him moving.

A few strides later, he managed to say, "I'll try."

By the time they reached the cluster of trees near the brewster's where Liam had suggested they meet, the sky had shifted from onyx to slate. A dozen men waited with sharpened sickles and scythes, a few burning torches held low, and more ready to blaze.

At the sight of Lana alongside him, the men fidgeted and murmured among themselves. Some gave her knowing looks, but most regarded her with startled suspicion. Only Liam hurried to greet them.

"I'd nearly given up," he whispered. His eyes flicked to Lana. Surely he recognized her; the community was too small to harbor anyone unfamiliar by sight, and Lana's bastard status had earned her more notoriety than most. But if her identity mattered to Liam, he didn't show it. Nor did he take any notice of the branches in her arms, although Aidan thought it considerably less likely that his brother knew anything of their significance.

"This will be no place for a woman not practiced as a warrior, Aidan," Liam said. "Have you changed your mind?"

"No."

"No one will think less of you if you have."

Aidan looked past the guttering glow of his nearly exhausted lamp to survey the dark faces of the men who awaited. Both Kyle and Michael stood among them. He supposed Liam was right, but he saw enough grim anticipation to know the makeshift mob would be disappointed if they lost their chance to teach a few Vikings a lesson.

Liam added, "And I would be much relieved to have one less grave to dig once the sun comes up."

Unable to bear his brother's heartfelt doubt, Aidan took refuge in jest. "Put me on a pyre with the Norsemen you kill, then."

Liam did not smile.

"Worry about staying out of your own grave," Aidan added gently. "I am going to do this."

Liam blew a long breath and looked back at Lana. "Send your friend on to the smithy, then."

"If she would listen to me, Liam, I might do that. But she won't. Lana is my . . . my wood-witch and she insists on going in with me."

Liam recoiled and turned wider eyes on her in a lengthy appraisal. His teeth dragged his lip, then he shook his head. Aidan could tell from the look on his face that his elder brother was going to call the whole thing off.

"She's too pretty to be very—"

Lana hissed. Both brothers jumped at the harsh sound, which would have befitted a spitting cat.

"Don't," Lana told Liam, her gritted teeth crushing the word to a growl. "Don't you dare question me. We have begun. It is too late to stop. If you are a man, I suggest you stand ready to kill them, because once I walk in, they will run out. Shrieking." With a final flash of her eyes, she turned on her heel and took a few steps toward the alehouse not far away.

The dumbfounded look on Liam's face would have

drawn a laugh from Aidan if the situation had been any less sober.

"Let's get this over with," Aidan said softly.

"Mother of God," Liam breathed, "I am glad she is on our side. When you appeared, I thought she was merely the one who was tempting you to . . ." He faltered, making the connection. "Aidan, for the love of the saints! Are you sure you know what you're doing?"

"No," Aidan said. "But I trust her. Let's go." He'd already said a few silent prayers on the way. Waiting would not make it easier. He did not want the quaking inside him to find its way out in visible form.

Liam stared at Lana's stiff back another long moment, then glanced over at the mob. Though all kept a nervous watch on Lana, several men nodded or gestured impatiently toward the alehouse. Liam exhaled hard, tipped his head in agreement, and then handed Aidan the curved blade of a scythe removed from its handle.

"Something that looks less like a weapon would be better," Aidan told him. "So they don't realize right away how I'm planning to use it."

Taking back the blade with a sour nod, Liam consulted a few of the men about their makeshift arms. Aidan settled on an iron hook for hanging pots over the hearth. He tucked it under his belt. It bounced on his thigh.

"Beware you are not caught in a spell," Liam murmured.

Then he grabbed the scruff of Aidan's neck and shook gently. "And come back out alive, little brother, whether you bring Brendan Donagh with you or not. We'll worry about his father when all else is done."

Aidan didn't argue. Resisting the urge to fling his arms around his brother, he thumped his fist on Liam's chest instead and then turned to catch up with Lana. He could soon hear the secretive rustle of men coming behind.

"Are you ready?" he asked her.

"We'll stop by the horse trough, in the shadow where nobody on watch could see us just yet," she said. "One or two things to do there. Then we'll go in. You still have your lamp?" She turned her head to check the sputtering flame.

"If the tallow will hold out a few moments more."

"We won't need it once we go through the door."

As they approached the brewster's, Aidan caught the round smell of beer and the grumble of conversation in the Norsemen's guttural language. The noise of many numbers and an occasional guffaw spilled out with the hearth light around the ill-fitting door. He tried to picture perhaps twenty men slouched around the fire, in every corner, and atop every table or bench. He mostly saw twenty swords and axes ready to go back to work after a long evening of rest.

Kyle darted up behind him and had Aidan and Lana wait while he and a few others skulked around the alehouse, trying to spot any guard or captives outside. Aidan took the chance to lift one hand and rest his fingertips on Lana's shoulder blade. He could not meet his fate without one last touch, however small and public and perhaps even unwanted.

She only turned her gaze on him and then back to the house, concentration plain on her face. But he thought she leaned into his hand.

He dropped it when Kyle returned with no news of activity outside the building. Brendan must be under close watch with his captors inside, where his noble blood gave them a confidence and security that Aidan hoped to prove false.

"Wait until you're inside to start torching the thatch?" Michael asked. Since Aidan's return, this brother had given no word of encouragement, doubt, or advice. He'd merely come up to stand silently beside him while they had waited on Kyle.

"No." Aidan's words scratched in his tight throat. "I want to go in after the fire catches but before they have noticed. Too much time will be worse than too little." He turned expectantly to Lana beside him.

She took a deep breath, then plucked three needles from the yew bough.

"Put these under your tongue," she whispered. "Don't swallow them, Aidan, they're poison. Just hold them there."

He obeyed, feeling as though she had given him some unholy communion. She did the same.

"The thatch?" she prodded.

Aidan nodded to the men. "Set the thatch alight. Quietly. Don't throw any torches atop yet." His fear thinned to a hazy relief. There was no turning back now.

While the men spread their flame among the torches and touched them to corners of the roof, Lana asked Aidan to hold out his flame as well. When he offered the lamp, she dipped the very tip of the yew in the flame. The needles began smoldering immediately. She closed her eyes and wafted the smoke into her face, inhaling deeply. When she opened her eyes again, a new, wild light shown there.

Gripping the holly in one hand and the sputtering yew in the other, she whispered, "And we enter, Aidan. The yew is alit. It will burn us to life or to death." She blew gently on the yew branch. To his surprise, the green bough burst into flame. For the first time, Aidan understood that his concern for her might be misplaced.

"Godspeed," Kyle whispered behind him. "To you both."

From nearby, Michael growled, "Don't make me come in after you, Aidan."

In a few paces, Aidan and Lana reached the door. She flung her hawthorn twig against the sill. She had assured him it could unlock as well as be kept sealed, and that it would loosen the door, even if it were bolted inside. He hadn't really believed her. Nonetheless, he followed the instructions she'd given and stomped the door as hard as he could with the flat of his heel, half expecting to break his foot against the strength of a bolt.

The door flew open. It bounced back and would have slammed shut again but that Aidan's force carried his whole body into the doorway. Flailing desperately to regain his balance, he stumbled to fall just inside the door. It struck him and stopped there, half open.

A chorus of startled grunts greeted him.

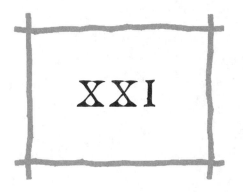

XXI

Aghast at his clumsy entrance into the alehouse, Aidan started to clamber to his feet. Someone kicked him back down. The foot pinned him there on his elbows and knees before he realized that it belonged to Lana. He could hear her shrieking at the top of her lungs. Her sounds might have been words, but not in any language he knew. He caught sight of a ring of stunned Viking faces. Then he remembered the plan. He'd almost ruined it, but she had responded quickly enough that the effect might have been even better. He whirled to cower and grovel at her feet as though more frightened of her than of the raiders. When he saw her livid face, he did not need to act much. Lana stood in the doorway, arms flung high, filling the space, both boughs aloft in her hands. The yew blazed; if she'd shifted it a few inches she could have set fire to the timbers herself.

By sheer force of will, Aidan scrunched his eyes almost

closed. He needed to spot any threatening motion, but he needed even more to focus on the humming of numbers. Flooded with people and shock, the room roared like the sea. Beer tankards dropped. He felt and heard Norsemen leaping to their feet, scattering dishes and toppling stools. The men instinctively grabbed for their weapons but didn't seem to know whether to use them.

Lana tapped Aidan's head with the holly as if anointing him. It drew his attention from numbers to her voice, and now he understood some of her words. Physically she ignored the Vikings, but clearly her banshee cries were directed at them.

"Vengeance for the dead, whom I summon and raise with the incense of this flaming Yew!" she shouted. "As you have dealt death to the living, thus will death be delivered to you! Tree of Life and of Death, see it done!" She snarled and screeched, making hideous sounds that echoed sickly in the tightness around Aidan's stomach.

Wrenching his attention back to the raiders, he listened for numbers. One by one, as Lana's shrieks filled the air, he isolated those of the men nearest him. None were easy to dismiss; all of the invaders were riled and filled with the day's bloodlust and conquest, and they hummed powerfully. Even numbers Aidan normally associated with temperance whirred and growled.

In the next instant he caught a firm, crooning eight, almost too calm in the havoc. He warned himself that just because Lord Donagh hummed of eight did not mean the Norse leader did, too. He knew from the sound's bold assurance, however, that he had found what he sought.

He converted a wave of relief into bellowing and gnarling. Still at Lana's feet, he barked like a dog, then slobbered and convulsed as if possessed by a demon. This act, meant to prove the fearsome power of witchcraft, sowed further confusion, to Aidan's relief. Men who had stepped forward now skittered back. They stood agape at Lana, probably not understanding a word but clear enough on her demonic fury and its apparent effect on the monk. Both scowls and emerging snickers gave way to horror.

Writhing, Aidan squirmed away from the door and toward that beckoning eight. Lana pursued him as though unaware of their audience, tapping at him with the holly. Men in blood-stained tunics stepped on one another's feet and crowded the walls, parting before Aidan and Lana. Terrified the same men would close around behind them and attack, Aidan roared and shivered more madly than ever. Finally he could reach out and claw at the high leather boots of the man he thought was their leader.

The Viking humming of eight did not retreat. He only

drew one foot back to kick off the demon-tormented monk. Aidan saw the blow coming well enough to take it in the shoulder instead of the head. Pain boosting his howls, he let the kick roll him back toward Lana. When she stepped over him, he knew she had understood.

Rolling his eyes madly, he caught sly glimpses of the room. He could see smoke curling down from the thatch, mingling with the haze that hung over the hearth. The brewster's guests hadn't noticed the new tendrils yet. They stood transfixed as Lana fearlessly directed her attention now to the man Aidan had tagged. Giving no ground, he glowered at her but did not yet lift a hand. The rest of his men watched to see how he would react. Their leader's response and the few seconds that followed would determine who lived and who died.

Aidan cast about desperately for Brendan Donagh. He spotted the brewster and his wife, two older boys bound to a heavy table in the back of the room, and a pile of tattered girls' garments that might have had a limp girl inside them. He prayed it was not his sister Regan. He did not see the lordling or anyone with sacking over his head.

Aidan rose half to his feet. For the moment the awe-struck Norsemen were still locked in the apprehension that a dead witch might be angrier and even more dangerous than a live one, since she might not be mortal at all.

Lana would not have more than a moment longer, however, before their leader or some other brave Viking decided to find out.

"Fire! Fire!" Aidan shouted in both his own tongue and Latin. Though he doubted the foreigners would understand either, he needed them to react to the burning thatch soon. He could smell it all the way down on the floor, so the flames had to be flashing and biting overhead.

The brewster took up the cry, dancing and pointing at the invading flames. The nearest Vikings eyed the rafters and pushed toward the door, suspicion twisting their features. They tightened their grips on their weapons. Their progress was hampered, however, by the rest of their fellows, whose attention remained fixed on Lana.

Weaving and flailing, Aidan dodged about in a crouch, desperately scanning the crowded room for the lord's son. He had met Brendan and knew the young lord hummed of seven, but there were many sevens here to sort out, amid much noise and confusion. Fear clutched his heart: Everything was taking too long. He would never survive, much less succeed, and Lana would die alongside him. Anguished, he glanced toward where she'd last stood.

"Haste, Aidan!" she shrieked, adding to the clamor. Before Aidan even recognized that demand was for him, she continued.

King Holly, do my work!
Take the will from those I strike!
Return the harm they've brought this place!
Pierce their hearts and pin their souls
with everlasting winter fire!

From the corner of his eye, Aidan saw her fling the burning yew into the air, scattering the men beneath where it fell. Then she slashed the Norse leader across the face, hard, with her holly bough.

"Thus may Holly blind thine eyes to better see thy path to death!" she roared.

Aidan cringed, horrified by what she'd just done and certain he would now witness her murder almost before he could move. To his great joy, the large fellow recoiled, blinked twice, and clapped his palms to his eyes. With a holler, he stumbled back into the arms of his men. Lana followed, whipping the holly branch in furious arcs against the surrounding faces. The leader's roar, whether curse or command or inarticulate wail, set the others in motion. Vikings stampeded like geese before a wolf, yelping. Flames licked near their heads.

Aidan dropped back to his knees as if in prayer and curled his head into his arms, perhaps the only person in the room not in motion. He had to block some of the confusion so that he might actually hear. The position triggered habit in him, and a silent plea rose from his heart up toward heaven.

There! The seven he sought purred subtly from the far side of the hearth.

Forgotten by the Norsemen in their panic over the wild witch and the new threat of burning, Aidan scrambled between slashing legs and around the glowing mound of coals. He found a body hunched nearby, a male body with cloth over his head. Brendan Donagh's smooth, resigned seven contrasted immensely with the room's tumult of numbers, all of which were now overlaid by the grating of terrified ones. Aidan had to respect that self-possessed seven.

"Stay still," he hissed into the sacking, thumping Brendan to make sure he heard and paid attention. "I'll set you free. Just a minute." The covered head nodded, so Aidan knew Donagh was alive and still conscious. His hands fumbled to remove the hood, held in place by snug coils of rope twined around the lordling's neck.

While his fingers scrambled, Aidan shot a glance around the room. He saw mostly wide backs. Norsemen surged toward the door, overturning benches on the way. Their tide swamped back at the threshold, where they swirled and shoved in their attempts to all get through at once.

Aidan's work also jammed: He couldn't loosen the

knot. Moving instead to Brendan's bound hands, he wished he'd brought the scythe blade after all. The lashed ropes were too tight to untie. Expecting someone to notice his efforts and begin raining down blows any moment, Aidan reached for the pothook at his belt.

It was gone. It must have fallen loose, unnoticed, when he'd stumbled at the door or squirmed and groveled thereafter. Aidan's legs wavered at the realization that he had crawled deep into a hornet's nest without any defense whatsoever. If he hadn't already been on the floor, he would have fallen.

He whirled to grab something, anything, that the brewster might have at his own hearth. The blank floor around the firepit mocked him. Even the hearth's iron firedogs were gone. The Norsemen had made sure that their hostage, though bound, could not grope for a weapon.

Abruptly, the jam at the doorway broke. Roaring men stomped out into the dark. A sudden fear gripped Aidan: Lana would either be trampled or swept out with them into a blade that didn't wait to make sure it was biting a raider. He had to find out exactly where she stood now. He jumped to his feet.

A bushy-bearded Viking at the back of the crowd, not expecting a young monk to rise into his path, slammed against Aidan. Reflexively, their glances met. The Norse eyes narrowed, seeing immediately that Aidan was not so possessed by demons as he had appeared. The big man raised the ax dangling in his hand.

Aidan leapt sideways. He only banged up short against an ale cask. In the instant before the man swung, Aidan knew he would die if that ugly blade hit him. He knew equally that the tables and benches and fleeing bodies around him did not grant him a place or a path to get out of its way. He grabbed an upended stool, aware that the weighty ax would smash through the wood and into him with barely a pause no matter how well he parlayed. Thuds and wails and murderous cries from outside the door told him his kin and their neighbors were busy. That must be satisfaction enough. Not wanting to watch the ax hit him, he swung the stool toward his opponent and swiveled his head to let his last sight be Lana.

She stood alone in a front corner of the house, glowering. The holly bough she held high before her like a fearsome green sword. Burning thatch rained around her. Even in their rush to escape from the fire, the Norsemen gave her wide berth.

As if she had felt Aidan's gaze, her face turned to him. She screamed his name.

The end of her cry was lost in a clatter and crash. The stool bashed from his grip, Aidan fell backward, stumbling over the captive he'd hoped to protect. He scrambled once more to his feet before he realized that he hadn't been knocked back by an ax in the chest. The two boys tied to the table in the back of the room had upended their anchor. Whether by fate, witchcraft, or chance, one corner had struck the threatening Viking's legs and knocked him to his knees, sending his ax blow astray along with the stool. Aidan smashed his heel into his enemy's bristling beard before the weapon could be lifted again. The man toppled and lay still.

Fire roared overhead, its heat growing intense. Aidan grabbed the ax and slashed its blade against the bonds of the two still struggling in panic with the table. They squirmed loose and lit out immediately.

Lana ran over to clutch him.

"Get to the door," he ordered, seeing the blazing house empty of raiders. "Take care it is safe before you go any farther. Run to Liam, if you see him. He'll protect you."

She took two steps before halting. Her eyes had crossed the pile that might have been a female captive. She ran and crouched to check.

Deciding he would get her out faster without argument, Aidan yanked Brendan Donagh to his feet. Still blinded and bound, the lord's heir shouted questions, but either composure or cowardice—it was hard to tell which—kept him from offering any struggle. Aidan hustled him toward the door and shoved him outside to the dirt of the yard. Young Donagh's ropes could be removed later, once Aidan had saved someone he cared about more.

He found Lana trying to get not one but two battered and frightened young women to their feet. His sister, Regan, when she recognized him, flung herself into his arms. He nearly carried her out, putting her down more gently than he'd managed for Brendan. Lana followed, guiding the other. Several men from the village, done swinging weapons and abruptly left with nothing to do, met them.

Aidan started again for the doorway, wreathed now in flame. Lana grabbed his arm.

"One more," he said, yanking loose and sprinting back to the threshold. If he took time to explain, the flames would make him too late.

Running crouched and coughing into the burning house, Aidan pulled the neck of his robe nearly to his eyes against the smoke. He could see almost nothing, but he thought he could get there by feel. He cracked his knee against the overturned table. Jerking away, he trod upon the Viking he'd downed, then stumbled and fell to his hands and knees at the hearth.

He felt the squeaky, dry crunch of coals under his left palm even before the burning began. Jerking away did not seem to make any difference. Pain screamed in his hand and fingers and wrist.

Moaning in agony, Aidan clutched his left hand to his chest, crawled away on his knees, and swept the far corner of the room with his right hand. Moments before, as he had seized the ax and cut the captive boys free, something else had registered in his overtaxed mind. A bundle of altar linens sat against the rear wall, revealed by the heaving aside of the table. Square corners had poked through the drape of the fabric. At least a few precious books might yet be recovered.

Aidan's fingers felt cloth. Not sure his burned hand would work right and certain he could not stand any increase in the pain, he used his left forearm and right hand to scoop up as much as he could reach of the linen and the weighty load wrapped within it. He trapped the chunky bundle against his body. Feeling volumes slipping and thudding away and knowing he had not gotten them all, he faced the hardest test he'd confronted all night. He floundered for an instant after lost books before his lungs refused to inhale the thick air again. He knew the dark smoke would claim him if he didn't go now. With a choked cry, he spun and made toward the door.

The floor was littered with debris and flame. Aidan never got to both feet for more than two steps before tripping again. He would not have made it over the threshold at all if Lana had not waited there for him, the holly branch still in her hand. As she drew him and his bundle to better air, smoke whirled in his head. He slipped into a half-conscious swoon in her arms.

The sensation of falling into blackness did not scare him. He felt confident that if he were bound not for sleep but for death, Lana would simply use her holly, God's evergreen token of mercy and rebirth, to raise him again.

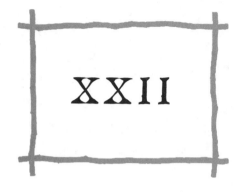

XXII

A roaring headache and a greater, tear-pricking fury in his left hand pulled Aidan back reluctantly to the world just a few heartbeats later. Somebody had borne him to the horse trough and doused him with cold water to quicken his spirit. Lana now held his wet head and shoulders in her lap, urgently calling his name and asking him questions long before he could understand any more than her voice.

He sat up, dizzy, and nearly wavered back over again. Just moving upright sent a rush of blood down his arm to his wounded hand. It answered with a fiery throb, forcing a cry through Aidan's clenched teeth. He curled protectively over his hand.

Lana pried it away from him to see what was the matter. When she saw the blisters and cracked skin, she yanked his whole arm to plunge his hand into the trough. Aidan closed his eyes and tried to breathe rather than gasp. The cold water helped.

"The Norsemen—all beaten?" he croaked, hoarse from the smoke.

"I think so," Lana said, before urging, "The yew needles, Aidan—if they're still in your mouth, spit them out."

He rolled his tongue to check. When he found them there, bitter, he did as she'd said.

"I thought for a moment they weren't going to protect you," she said, her voice trembling. "That beast with the ax . . ."

Aidan nodded, too wrapped in pain to feel much triumph or relief. Eager for any distraction, he managed, "Lucky the table tipped when it did."

"I believe in forces larger than luck," she replied. "You may thank the boys and the table. I'll thank the yew. And your numbers."

Her words recalled the maelstrom of noise and confusion through which they'd just passed. A shiver rippled Aidan's skin at the memory of that test, but having met it gave him new confidence, and not just in himself. The humming of numbers, steadfast amid chaos, reassured him that an order existed beneath the surface of the world, one he could hear and have faith in.

Wary of succumbing to pride, he told Lana, "Perhaps God deserves the most credit."

She stroked his arm where it stretched over the side of the horse trough. "Is that not what I just said?"

Liam approached through the smoke. Aidan pushed himself shakily to his feet. The dawn light showed his older brother so drenched with blood, Aidan feared that some of it must belong to Liam.

"Are there wounds under that blood?" he demanded, reaching to check for himself.

"None I can feel," Liam replied. "Better tend to your own." He pointed, not to Aidan's hand but to the front of his robe.

Aidan looked down. A long rip marred his robe over the top of one thigh, high enough to have sliced the thin tunic beneath, too. The Viking with the ax had not missed completely. A bit of blood oozed. Now that Aidan knew it had cause, his leg hurt, although more with the ache of a blow than the sting of a slice. He fumbled with the torn fabric to see how much worse it looked underneath.

"I already checked," Lana told him. " 'Tis not so much more than a bruise and a scratch."

"You already—" Aidan faltered, turning red at the liberty she had taken while he had been absent from his body.

Liam laughed.

"I saw nothing immodest," she protested. "Just the wound on your leg!"

"Call yourself blessed and thank God, little brother," Liam told him. "I truly expected to mourn your bold heart.

But even from outside, we were cowed." He gave Lana an appreciative look openly tinted with fear. "I hope your rage has been spent, dread maiden."

Lana stared at her hands, her face drawn in dismay. "Not 'dread,'" she whispered.

"Liam." Uncharacteristic iron edged Aidan's voice. "Her name is Lana, and I don't want a word said against her."

"Nor shall one be," Liam said. "I'll make certain of that. After what she has just done for us, with such unspoken cunning, no one would dare." His brow creased, however, and he stepped nearer Aidan to whisper, "I know who she is, Aidan, and whose daughter, too. But I saw her striking at them as they ran out the door. Those scratched by her holly could barely raise arms or see their way to run." Giving Aidan a pointed look, he added, "Be wary of her."

Lana must have heard that, for amusement battled with the regret on her face.

Despite the holly's enfeebling effect, the villagers had not come away from their ambush unscathed. One man was dead. Another had received a gut wound, and although he was on his feet, laughing, they all knew it would likely take poison in the next days and kill him.

"Kyle?" Aidan looked about in the dawn light for dear faces. "Michael?"

"Both sound," Liam assured him. "Michael took a fair nick on one arm, but it should heal. He's with Regan."

Their sister and the other young woman who had huddled with her had been terrified and abused, but they would survive. The alehouse shimmered in flames. Neither the brewster nor his wife voiced a complaint. They knew others had suffered more, and all were relieved to say the raid was over at last. Not a Norseman had escaped, and Liam planned to let them lie where they'd fallen for Lord Donagh to find.

"Should we hie away from here, then?" Aidan asked his brother. The sunrise was beginning to rival the fire. "Is it wise to be here when he appears?"

"I don't see why not, since his own blood did not spill." Liam jerked his head. Brendan Donagh had been released of his bonds and now strolled among the corpses, spitting on faces and thrusting one of the Vikings' own weapons into their motionless flesh. The two brothers watched dubiously.

"He should have shown that much spirit before the bag went over his head," Liam muttered.

Aidan shrugged. Having accounted for the people he cared about most, he wanted to check something else.

The bundle of books lay not far away. Aidan cradled his scorched, dripping hand and went to inspect them.

"I didn't get this far, did I?" he asked Lana, beside him. "Someone dragged it away from the reach of the flames."

"I did," she said, "while they hauled you to the trough. I knew it must be important to you."

He slid aside the wrappings that belonged on the altar. Eight books lay beneath, including several Gospels and a fine Book of Hours. Although their bindings had no rich metals to scavenge, the raiders must have realized that their finely wrought illumination would fetch a price worth carting them off. These eight were but a fraction of the abbey's former collection, and any remainders were charred vellum by now. Still, Aidan touched their tooled covers and felt pleased with himself. Eight books were much better than none. Starting over from scratch would have required the scribes to disperse to other monasteries for as long as two years before they could bring any new copies home.

He didn't object when Lana turned a few pages and ran her fingertips over the gold-inked illumination.

A shadow from the breaching sun fell over them both. Aidan looked up. Brendan Donagh stood there. Aidan rose, mindful that the fray was over and he'd better now show the usual respect. Brendan was not guaranteed his father's position, but wealth and force and dynastic intrigue made his selection almost that certain.

In the meantime, no more hissing or thumping would be tolerated.

"I'm told that I owe my liberation to you," Brendan said.

Uncomfortable, Aidan shrugged. "And to others," he said, keeping his eyes low.

"I'm not the fool I may look," Brendan told him. "I surrendered to them to save the lives and honor of my mother and sisters. I knew they'd want ransom more than they wanted to kill me, and my father could provide it."

"You owe me no explanations, lordship," Aidan said. Brendan's powerful seven hummed and scratched in his ears. The young lord obviously felt defensive, and Aidan might not have made the same choices. Yet the fellow was neither stupid nor weak, his number confirmed that, and he would be no man to thwart once his father was gone.

"If I or my father can repay your courage, I would like to hear how."

Aidan tipped his head. "If my family has need, perhaps I may ask in the future." The young lord might remember the offer when tribute was due or drought ruined a crop. "Many thanks."

Brendan nodded but did not step away. Wondering if his answer had not been enough, Aidan peeked up. He discovered the lordling gazing down at Lana, who still crouched near Aidan's feet. Not only had she not risen courteously, she did not look up from the books. The whites of her knuckles gleamed against the colorful pages. Instinct, still primed from battle, told Aidan that fury, not fear, clenched those fists. He felt himself grow tense in response.

"I thought I recognized your screeching," said Brendan Donagh, a smirk on his face.

Lana rose abruptly, staring Brendan right in the face only long enough to deliberately turn her back and walk away.

Surprise and trepidation hoisted Aidan's eyebrows. He glanced back at Brendan.

Still smiling slyly, Brendan rolled his eyes to meet Aidan's. He did not seem to mind either Lana's disrespect or Aidan's inquiring look.

"I've tasted that saucy fruit," Brendan said, raising his voice so that she would still hear him. "'Tis a pity you are a monk. You can't take full advantage."

In the instant before Aidan realized what he meant, he merely frowned at the gleam in young Donagh's sharp eyes. Then the mockery hit hard against something he already knew.

From where he stood, the quickest blow with his uninjured fist was a backhanded slash. Brendan stumbled back. The shock, pain, and outrage on his face so satisfied Aidan that he leapt after the nobleman to hit him again. He was only sorry his left hand hurt too much to help.

Kyle, nearby, heard the thud of fist on flesh, or perhaps Lana's yelp of dismay. He dragged Aidan off before he'd done too much damage or taken any in return. Liam and others quickly clustered around.

"Soft, friend," Kyle said amiably, getting Aidan under control. "We already know you've gone mad and admire you for it. But why beat on someone you just risked your life for? Is this something they teach at the abbey?"

When Aidan's anger had ebbed enough for him to reply, he growled, "Yes. I'm beating a bit of the sin out."

He glared while Brendan regained his composure. The witnesses carefully looked elsewhere. The young lord dabbed at the bloodied and already swelling parts of his face. He scowled at Aidan, and they locked eyes a long time.

"I believe anything I may owe you has just been repaid," Brendan said softly.

Aidan found several retorts, but Kyle gripped his right arm with enough force to numb everything beneath those clamped fingers. Aidan took his friend's silent advice and said nothing.

Brendan nodded thoughtfully, then turned and strode swiftly away without another glance at Lana or anyone else.

Liam cuffed Aidan so hard across the back of the head that Kyle had to help him keep his feet.

"He could have had you blinded for that!" Liam said. "What were you thinking?"

"Nothing," Aidan replied. "Just that I will never make a monk."

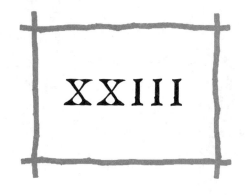

XXIII

Lana said not a word about Brendan or the fisticuffs. Once the others had turned away, Aidan drew her close. She merely clutched him and hid her face in his sleeve. He could feel her shame through her trembling hands. Having seen what she'd done in the alehouse, he wondered why she'd never punished her half brother with some kind of hex. Aidan knew not to ask. He held her instead.

In pain and abruptly exhausted, he decided not to wait for the elder Lord Donagh to appear. Aidan asked Lana if she wanted him to walk her downriver to her mother's cottage.

"No," she said. "First I want to make a birch poultice for your poor hand. We can do that at the creek. Then I want to go back to the holly and see if it would keep my rowan charm. You should come with me."

Aidan wearily wiped his face with his sleeve. "What I should do is take the manuscripts back to the abbey."

"They've been gone overnight. Another hour or two won't make a difference. Leave them with your kin."

Too tired to argue and longing for the searing in his hand to subside, he gave in. Before they left, Lana thrust the raw end of the battered holly branch into the ground near the horse trough.

"If it takes root it will bring powerful luck to the brewster," she explained. "He'll need some."

"I thought holly brought ill luck except on the Yule."

"It wasn't unlucky for you, was it? You have to know how to wield it."

Aidan studied her face, recalling the dreadful apparition she'd made with a blazing bough in one hand and a holly sword in the other.

"You were astounding, Lana," he said softly. His heart squeezed down on itself in an unfamiliar and vaguely frightening way. "Terrifying and astounding."

She looked at the ground, licking her lips. "I've never hurt anyone like that before," she mumbled. "Even if they were invaders."

He touched her elbow. "You did right. They would have gone on to kill many more somewhere else."

"Will my soul burn for it, though?"

Aidan knew how he wanted to answer, but not what heaven's answer would be. Thinking of the newly dead villager and the injured one likely to join him, he ached as though he'd dealt their fatal blows himself. If he had never sunk the longboats, probably both men would have welcomed next week. Yet he didn't see how a person could take action at all if he stood trembling in fear of the unknowable future.

"If any soul needs the purification of fire for tonight's work," he decided, his stomach clenching, "it is mine. Yet Christ spoke of forgiveness. I will pray hard that God may grant it to you. Perhaps His grace will extend also to me."

The concern on her face did not vanish, but an uncertain smile lightened it. She cupped the back of his burned hand. "You've already been in the fire," she said. "I'll hope that was enough."

Lana dressed Aidan's seared hand with a mash of wet, crumpled birch leaves and moss. The cool, soft cushion soon muffled the bolts of pain being thrown up his arm. She decided to hold the poultice in place with a strip ripped from the hem of her chemise.

"My undershift is already torn," he offered. "Want to use that?"

"You can't tear a decent strip with only one hand, can you?" she asked.

"No, but you probably—" He stopped at the picture that rose in his mind. The potential embarrassment in lifting the hem of his robe up his bare thighs or fishing through its new rip daunted them both. Lana blushed. Neither said anything more about his idea.

Lana had only to curl the border of her long shift a few inches to tear at the fabric beneath. Though he'd seen plenty of legs while working the fields, Aidan found himself fascinated by his glimpses of hers. When she struggled, he wanted to help. He thought better of it.

As she gently tied the strip around his useless hand, he studied her face and wondered what she would do. Even if she still surrendered herself to the abbey, as she'd agreed to do just the previous afternoon, Aidan no longer believed a stone penitent's cell would hold her. Perhaps her part in repaying the raiders—and saving the ransom— might move Lord Donagh to pardon her. Freed, she could return to her mother. Aidan felt a stab of selfish sorrow at that hope.

He thought about his own future, too, as they made their way back to the holly bush they'd visited in the dark hours before dawn. Brother Nathan's scriptorium would bear Aidan's mark; the books he had saved ensured that. But could he bear the abbey's mark upon him? He pondered going back to unhurried movements, downcast eyes, obedience, silence. The monastery promised rest and peace. Although at the moment he longed for both, he feared a monk's life, for him, would also bring numbness.

When she spotted the holly, Lana gave a cry and ran ahead. Her rowan charm lay on the ground beneath the branch where she'd hung it.

She scooped it up and spun to him, beaming. Her eleven rose and sang.

"Look! The holly has given my charm back. That means we don't owe it anything more. It is satisfied with our use of its wood."

He smiled, more pleased by her jubilance than whatever relief he should feel. While she drew the red yarn back over her neck, Aidan gnawed at his lips and tried to make a decision. Looking back down the hill toward the monastery, and seeing instead everything that had passed since they'd both been inside its ramparts, he realized abruptly that most of his choice had already slipped past him. He had spent a year of apprenticeship in the abbey, and years of study before that, and the events of a single night had swept him too far downriver to return.

The same events had swept him elsewhere, though, and he was not there alone.

He caught Lana's hand and drew it to his chest. The girlish joy on her face mellowed to something richer but also more uncertain. She leaned into him. The hum of eleven about her leapt with a harmonic of hope.

Aidan brushed his lips against her eyelids and the bridge of her nose, but he forced himself to stop there. If his lips fell upon hers, he knew the Naught of her kiss would completely empty his mind, and he had something he wanted to say, or to ask. If he did not set it loose soon, it would cower inside him until more reasoned thoughts battered it into regret.

"Lana, listen to me," he pleaded, when her free hand glided up his arm to his shoulder, urging his face back toward hers.

The earnestness in his voice gave her pause. She drew back a half step.

Aidan closed his eyes to ask for some grace. Deprived of the sight of her face, they sprang open again.

"I'm sure I am not under the proper tree, or the moon is not right, or everything's wrong," he began. The words tumbled from his lips and seemed to skitter away, unchecked, into the long morning shadows. "I can't help it. And I know that you haven't known me for long, Lana, but it feels as though you've known me fairly, and I am . . . bewitched by you, truly. So I guess with God's help what I mean to say is—Lana, would you be my wife?"

Her mouth fell open before she caught it up and made it work more correctly. "But . . . what of the abbey?"

He looked down between them, acutely aware of the dirt and blood and violence marking his robe. "With my father and Gabriel gone," he said softly, "there will be enough O'Kirin cattle for me." He gulped back both sorrow and guilt, feeling as though he were treading on graves that had not even been dug yet. He and Gabriel had been close, though, and Aidan knew that Gabe would approve of him taking his place. "I haven't asked Liam or Michael yet, of course," he amended, "but I am certain they will not object. And so many have been killed that the clan will be forced to hold a gaveling soon, to redistribute the land, and I can get a share of my own."

After a worrisome silence, he added, "I will ask your mother, your uncle, or even your father for your hand if you like. 'Tis your answer that matters first, though."

"Oh, Aidan," she murmured. Then she fell quiet again. He could barely raise his eyes to her face, afraid of finding disdain, or worse, amusement. He steeled himself and met her gaze.

"Yes," she said, having waited for that. "I will and with honor, if you don't change your mind." Apprehension tainted her happy glow. "But what about your books? What about being a scribe?"

He tried to ignore the knot between his stomach and throat. "I don't think I can do it," he managed, forcing the words out. "I'm not sure I could have taken the vows in good faith even if I had not met you. And now all that has happened, all that I feel . . ." He shook his head help- lessly.

She stepped closer again and raised her free hand to

stroke his where it still held the other to his chest. "You know how to read regardless. If you'll chop the wood, I will help you make tablets from beech. Beech wood is smooth and full of ideas, and it holds on to knowledge. It is perfect for writing. You can make books of your own."

Trying to smile at her innocent suggestion, he did not lay out the reasons he couldn't. He just raised both her hands and pressed his lips to her knuckles. They wanted to explore her hands farther, but he made them talk yet.

"Tomorrow is Sunday," he said. "After Mass I will ask Father Niall—" A fear struck him. "If he's still alive, anyway, I will ask if he would sanctify our marriage."

"Our handfasting," she added, squeezing his fingers. A dreamy anticipation lit her face.

Reluctant to disturb that joy but unable to press back a worry, Aidan said, "I'm not sure if a bastard's father has the right to approve any match, but yours often takes liberties that aren't rightly his. Do you think he will object to me?"

She snorted. "He won't care. You just saved both his son and his ransom. Besides, I can always renounce the inheritance that the law says I should get. He'd be delighted to keep that as a bride-price."

"I don't deserve a bride that costly," murmured Aidan, both relieved and appalled.

"Don't make me slap you," she said, softening the words with a smile. Then a startled look crossed her face.

"My mother certainly has to approve, though!" Her concern shifted quickly back to a grin. "Though 'tis hard to see how she could object to a monk."

Aidan said gently, "I won't be a monk for much longer. I'll just be a herdsman and a tiller of land." It hurt even more to say to her than to admit to himself. He grimaced in apprehension of relating that decision to those left at the abbey.

They parted there in the woods. Lana would not hear of him taking her back to her mother's cottage that day. She wanted to present him as a suitor, preferably one not wearing a monk's robe streaked with blood. He understood. He didn't mind missing the extra walk, either. Hunger had begun to gnaw through his exhaustion and he wanted to beg a few bites from Liam, return the manuscripts he'd saved, and be done with whatever trial he might face with the monks.

Aidan found the abbey mercifully free of corpses. The grating sound of the number one, that buzz of fear and pain and dread that had echoed the last time he'd been here, had faded. Kinder, more familiar numbers had replaced it, prompting a twinge of nostalgia he hadn't expected. He hesitated just inside the front gate, braced for shouts or expulsion. The few monks within view only looked, saw he posed no threat, and continued their scrubbing of blood.

Not sure where to go first, he glanced into the open

doorway of the dead abbot's chamber as he passed. It was not empty, as he had assumed it would be. Brother Nathan kneeled in the corner, his hands clasped in prayer.

Aidan stopped and stood in the doorway a moment, unsure what to do. He did not want to interrupt devotions, but the door yawned wide open, and Brother Nathan was the person he most wanted to see.

While he debated whether to speak or walk on, Brother Nathan heard his rustling presence. He opened his eyes.

"Brother Aidan," he said. "I was not sure we would see you ag—" He froze, taking in the fabric-wrapped bundle clasped to Aidan's chest.

"I've mostly come to return these," Aidan said, hurrying to rest his load on the table. "Did you hear what took place at the brewster's?"

"We heard." Brother Nathan's somber expression made Aidan wonder which details the monk knew. He supposed, given his errand, it made little difference.

Nathan continued, "The messenger did not mention, however, that any of God's stolen riches had been retrieved." He rose quickly from the corner to lay his hands on the altar cloths. As he drew the fabric aside, the old monk uttered a dry gasp.

" 'Tis only a few, the rest were hacked apart for their bindings or burned," Aidan said, apologetic. Brother Nathan did not answer. He ran his hands over the leather-bound volumes, quickly sliding them left and right to see which books had been saved. Even after he'd touched each one twice, his hands hovered, trembling, over their covers.

"I think," he said, sinking very slowly onto his stool, "you had better explain your part in this merciful bounty from God."

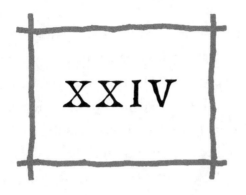

XXIV

Aidan told Brother Nathan in broad strokes what he had done since he'd run out of the chapel the night before. He managed to do so without mentioning Lana, only describing the events at the alehouse as a vengeful attack by the villagers. Brother Nathan might very well know the whole story already, but Aidan would not be the one to bring up her name or anything she had done.

As he talked, he fought a distraction. He'd spotted a few fragments of wood in the corner. Roughly the size of spoons, they'd caught his eye because he could hear them humming numbers far too low for wood. He realized they must be the discarded wood rods Lana had been trying to pawn to pilgrims. Remembering that she had wanted them back, he hoped he would get a chance to retrieve them for her, either with or without Brother Nathan's permission.

When Aidan finished speaking, Brother Nathan tapped two fingers against his lips.

"I cannot tell you how grateful I am," the old monk said finally. "My prayers have been answered in a way I thought impossible." His eyes narrowed at Aidan. "One of my prayers, at least. Tell me, Brother Aidan, how another will be answered. You have been blatantly disobedient and absent from this monastery for nearly a full day. How shall I view your return? Shall I call Brother Eamon and give him the glad news that he still has a novice to ward?"

Aidan focused on the pain in his left hand to avoid the tingling shame that coursed through the rest of his body. He couldn't raise his eyes off the table.

"I still long with all my heart to serve as a scribe, Brother Nathan," he said, when he trusted his voice. "But I have realized that my devotion may be too weak for me to be a good monk."

"Or your own will too strong, perhaps," Nathan remarked.

Closing his eyes, Aidan just nodded.

Nathan rose from his stool. Aidan flinched, not sure what to expect, but the old monk simply walked past to stand at his door, looking out. Aidan kept his face toward the wall.

"Your honesty, at least, pleases heaven," Nathan said from behind him. "I am forced to agree. Yet I hesitate to release a novice whom God has directed to restore our library."

Taken aback, Aidan listened to Brother Nathan's nine

humming an intricate harmony against the hush in the room. An imaginative spirit coiled inside that number. Hearing it, Aidan decided he had nothing to lose.

"I have not heard of it done," he said to the table, "but might your scriptorium ever admit a lay scribe?"

"I cannot allow profane hands to set down God's holy Word," Brother Nathan replied immediately, his tone clipped.

"Of course not," Aidan murmured. "I'm sorry." He had thought, when he had asked his question, that little hope lay behind it. The distance his heart now fell made it clear he'd been fooling himself. He let his fingers say good-bye to the books on the table before him. His hand shook.

Then he cleared the lump from his throat and added, "Should I see Brother Eamon before I go?" He wanted desperately to bury his dreams and escape.

"Not yet."

Aidan clenched his jaw and waited to see what else Brother Nathan might say. The monk did not move from the doorway. The silence stretched on so long, Aidan would have thought Brother Nathan had departed if not for the lyric nine zinging behind him.

Finally he peeked over his shoulder to check whether Brother Nathan was even looking at him. The senior monk leaned against the door frame, his eyes closed, his head bent, and his hands folded in prayer.

Confused, Aidan fidgeted. Brother Nathan's instructions to remain, however, had been clear. While the failed novice watched and wondered what to do, the elder monk flashed his hawk's eyes open once more.

"I am not abbot yet," Brother Nathan told Aidan. "It is likely, however, that I will be, unless our good Lord Donagh has more kin in need of a post."

Wondering why Nathan even mentioned his own authority, Aidan concluded it must herald the declaration of some punishment or price for renouncing the life of a monk. He steeled himself to hear it.

"I will remain the scriptorium's master regardless," Nathan continued. "We have more empty tables today than we did yesterday. Yet God's grace has ensured that the scribes who remain need not sit idle." Leaving the doorway to return to his seat, he gave Aidan an inscrutable look from beneath his woolly gray brows.

"I cannot allow profane hands to copy God's Word," Nathan repeated, "but decoration, perhaps, might not always require the tonsure. Vines and borders and humble creatures are part of God's work but not, strictly speaking, His Word. A lay brother might serve as a colorist or illuminator. Or a copyist of our two remaining profane works." His gaze slid briefly to the books on the table before returning to Aidan. "If the circumstance were unusual enough."

Aidan tried to draw a breath. His chest refused to permit it. He must have misunderstood.

"And if he could be trusted never to step over the bounds he was given," Nathan added. "On pain of expulsion, with no second chance. Could you bow to such constraint? Obedience has not been your strength."

His eyes wide, Aidan started to reply jubilantly. He'd always been more drawn to illumination than text, and most scribes specialized in one or the other anyhow. Whatever bounds Nathan drew would be spacious compared to losing the opportunity forever. And the abbey's expectations of those who would never take perpetual vows and the tonsure were light enough to bear, especially knowing he could throw them off again every eve—

A thought struck him. He hid his face in his good hand. "I guess I cannot," he moaned. "I have asked someone to become my wife, just this day, and she has accepted." He imagined telling Lana that he'd changed his mind. Although he thought she might understand, he couldn't face the full weight of the guilt and loss that wrenched at him now, just considering it. He still wanted Lana, even knowing the price. "I'm sorry, Brother Nathan," he added. "Only heaven knows how much. But I can't turn my back on that pledge. Or on her."

His eyebrows crowding his hair, Brother Nathan rubbed

his weathered jaw. "I must say you have been remarkably busy since you left to gather oak apples, Aidan," he said. "And you are wise to recognize the gravity of your commitment. But I do not see any objection per se. A lay brother is not a monk in holy orders, and while many live here with us by the rules of this house, others vow chastity as a voluntary virtue. Members of the laity are not bound either as residents or bachelors."

Aidan could not believe his ears or God's grace.

"Besides," Brother Nathan said dryly, "you know as well as I do that some of our clergy, and monks in too many lax houses, take Saint Paul's advice against wives rather lightly. I will ask only that you behave as discreetly as possible. You are here by the Hour of Prime and remain through Vespers, just as servants and all lay brothers do. And she does not enter this abbey except to worship at the High Cross like any other Christian woman. I reserve the right to rescind this privilege, Aidan, and I will do so immediately if my heart ever tells me that God does not approve."

Aidan would have remained there giving thanks until sunset if Brother Nathan had let him.

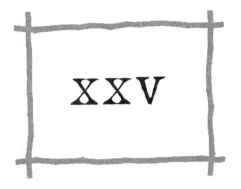

XXV

In his excitement, Aidan almost forgot Lana's wood. When he remembered, just outside the doorway, he stuck his head back inside and meekly asked Brother Nathan if it would do any harm for him to take it.

The senior monk raised one eyebrow and gave Aidan the most scrutinizing stare of his life. He felt as though Brother Nathan were seeing him unclothed.

"I told them you would never withstand that temptation," Brother Nathan said. "I tried to distract you. I see how soundly I failed. But I suppose the truth is better known sooner than later. I hope you will take it upon yourself to lead your bride, once she is yours, nearer to God."

Having no intention of repaying Nathan's generosity with a lie, Aidan licked his lips and said, "I will try, Brother Nathan." He didn't expect to succeed.

"At least ensure that she does not lead you farther from Him. If I see that, our agreement will end."

"Of course," Aidan assured him.

Nathan's gaze shifted to the wood on the floor. "Can I trust that this . . . kindling will trouble pilgrims, Lord Donagh, and this abbey no more?"

"I swear it."

Brother Nathan waved at the sticks. "Take it and begone, then. I expect you to find a clean robe and a few hours of sleep and to stand at the High Cross with the lay brethren by Prime in the morning. You can begin your new life fittingly with the Mass."

Aidan cradled the wood to his heart and pondered its humming all the way back to Lana's uprooted tree. He wasn't sure she would be there, but she had offered to return before sunset in the hope that he could also return and share the results of his trial. Though he tried to run, his feet dragged in weariness and he stumbled over painful memories of lost family and friends. He wondered, aching with loss and guilt, if those dreadful deaths had somehow funded his recent good fortune. As excited as a part of him felt, he would not have chosen the trade.

Hearing his crackling footsteps, Lana ducked from behind the hawthorn to greet him. She crowed at the sight of her wood in his hand.

"You brought it!" Not even taking it from him, she jumped to plant kisses all over his cheeks.

"You must promise not to sell it, or work mischief with

it, or even discuss it with anyone," Aidan warned, trying to cover all possibilities.

"I promise you," she said soberly. "Can you feel it?"

He nodded, giving over her treasures. "I can't understand it, but I see why you think it is special. It hums of eleven as well, and other numbers, all primes." Outside the abbey, Aidan had inspected the age-polished wood, listening as closely as he could. He heard seventeen and thirteen and the same bright and trickish eleven that he thought of as belonging to Lana. Perhaps she would show him where she had found it. He doubted that fragments of Christ's crucifix had traveled so far from the Holy Land, or that their bearer would have lost them if they had. He would not be surprised, though, to learn that these lumps of wood had some other connection to power—fragments from the ship of Saint Brendan the Voyager or the staff of Saint Patrick or the Briton King Arthur's great table. He expected Lana would puzzle it out eventually.

As she danced in joy, the sticks clasped in her hands, he told her his own happy tidings. She cheered—then pouted.

"That means I will see you only at night," she said.

"And Sunday," he reminded her. "The scribes do not work then. Winter nights are coming, though, Lana. They may be cold, but they're long." With effort, he quashed the grin that wanted to arise at the prospect of long nights with her.

She pursed her lips and tapped them with a piece of her wood. "Aidan, I am so happy for you, and I will accept nights without days. Please don't misunderstand me. But if I do have to renounce my inheritance, and you create books all day long, how will I eat? And suppose we have children? Can you bring food home for us?"

Aidan stiffened, dismayed by how poorly he had thought this all through. He'd been so amazed by Brother Nathan's offer, and so weary, that his mind had not been working clearly.

Then the answer arrived, belatedly. It brought relief wrapped in heartache.

"We'll still live in my father's cottage," he told her. He thought of the work his mother had done there, and it hurt. "You can help Regan and Gabe's wife prepare food and tend the animals. My brothers would never let them starve, nor will you."

A glimmer of hope shone on her face before being trampled by her dogged practicality. "Sooner or later they'll have wives of their own, though," Lana said. "Wives who will want to take over the house and the fruits of their husbands' labors."

As difficult as it was for him to imagine Liam with a new wife, Aidan knew she was right. He nodded, untroubled. His mind had already traced a few other options.

"The animals are the crux, though, Lana, not the house. A sod house can go up in a few days. You and Sarah can till my land share together, or we can trade some of the oxen for more milk cows and ewes so you can make butter and cheese. Decent cows will yield enough extra to trade. I'll bring home what I can and do chores in the dark if need be. Either way, I dare say you'll eat better than you have until now."

The strain on her face broke. "That wouldn't be hard," she said. "And I am happy to work for my keep like anyone else. But I don't know much about cows."

"You'll learn. You've learned your mother's lessons, obviously."

She set her wood carefully down at the base of a tree. Her deliberate manner made Aidan think she was angry or changing her mind about becoming his wife. He watched, apprehensive, as she walked back to face him and took his uninjured hand in both of her own.

"I may be able to trade as a midwife as well, once my mother is gone," Lana said softly. "If you will not prohibit it."

Aidan drew a deep, careful breath. "I will make sure you don't need to," he said. "I can't have the monks know my wife is a witch." They would hear rumors regardless, of course. Brother Nathan's hard staring that morning implied that they already had. There were limits, however, to what men could ignore.

"Monks don't need midwives, so they won't find out." Her sly grin lit her face. Aidan fought a swell of terror, wondering what trouble he was sowing for himself.

His fear subsided in the wash of her singing eleven. It surged when she smiled, and Aidan's doubts were drowned out by the strength and hope and mystery of that hum.

Lana squeezed his fingers and asked, "Do you have to return to the abbey right away?"

When he told her he was free until the morrow, she drew him by the hand.

"Come sit here with me on the moss, then."

She inspected his burned hand and added a few more birch leaves that she chewed and moistened with her spittle. Aidan felt like a kitten receiving a bath from its mother. He thought of his own mother, alive yesterday and now dead, and he swallowed hard against the sting in his throat before it could rise to prick childish tears.

When Lana was done, she did not let go of his hand.

"I wanted to tell you something," she said. Her gaze remained on her handiwork but a smile played on her lips.

Aidan tried to keep breathing. So many of the things she said made him nervous. He wondered if that was why his heart often quivered in her presence.

When she raised her eyes to his and their blue weight fell on him, his stomach flopped. As tired and heartsick as he was, that look made him forget it.

"Do you remember the first time I saw you?" she asked.

"When I gave you the rose?"

"No, before that. When I first arrived at the abbey."

"When you were dragged in, you mean," Aidan teased. He recalled more than her unwilling entry, however. When her eyes had first fallen on him, she had looked startled and then inexplicably annoyed.

"Hush," she admonished. "Never mind that. I recognized you. I lied later on when I said that I hadn't."

"I could tell," he told her. "But why?"

"I didn't recognize you from the village. I once scryed your face."

Aidan rolled his shoulders to cover a shiver. He did not like the idea that his image had appeared in any witching water.

"Don't you want to know why you appeared in my scrybowl?" she prodded.

"I'm afraid to."

She giggled and reached to tweak his chin, making him feel like a small boy even as his skin wished her hand would linger and touch more. He decided again that claiming her as his own would be worth the discomfort.

She said, "I was scrying the face of the man I would

marry. I didn't know whose face it was, because you spent so much time with the monks, I suppose. But when I discovered you there at the abbey, in a robe, I thought my scrying must have been false." Her mouth curved in a self-satisfied grin. "I'm rather pleased it was true."

Conflicted, Aidan inhaled the thick scent of the moss beneath them. Its lively, thirty-ish hum reassured him. He told himself that if God's divine plan aligned him with a witch, then better a skilled one than a clumsy one.

"What else haven't you told me?" he wondered.

Her saucy gaze fell away. The hand holding his tightened, and he could feel that she did it to conceal a tremor. Glad he could unsettle her in return, he pressed, "Be fair to me, Lana. If we're to be bound together, it is my right to know."

"When you touched me last night," she said softly, "and I stopped you, I was sorry I had."

Her words and the memory shot a hot spike low into his belly. This was not the sort of confession he had expected. Uncertain what reply she would want and afraid of giving a wrong one, he stayed silent. He only reached a finger to trace the red yarn of her rowan charm where it curled around the side of her neck. His fingertip slipped insolently under the yarn. Aidan wished it were the collar of her shift.

She murmured, "I was just scared, Aidan."

Her eyes contained the same anxiety now. He could see something else plain, though, and perhaps more important, that she did not say: Last night, she had needed to know she *could* stop him.

With effort he pulled his hand from her neck and clenched it in his lap. "As much as you scare me," he said, "I don't want to scare you. Not like that. And I don't want to make you think of . . . of anyone who has hurt you."

She didn't respond, only gazed at him, but he lost track of her eyes for her lips. They pressed together, then parted, then seemed to beg him to kiss them.

He gave them what they, and he, wanted. Lana did not react as if she were scared.

Their kiss blurred into a harmony of warm breath and soft gasps and heartbeats and not enough skin. Then a stone poked Aidan's ribs, and probably Lana's, as he lay back with her on the moss. The nip of pain sliced through the thundering None that rolled through his head when they touched. It returned him briefly to himself. He realized what he was about to do if she did not stop him . . . again.

He shook his head to clear it and pushed himself back upright.

She remained prone on the moss, only shifting to avoid the sharp edge of the rock. She watched him.

"I'm sorry," he said. "You take all of my will from me

except for one thing. But we can stand at the door of the church soon enough. I can wait if I know it will not be forever."

Although his voice sounded firm in his ears, he could not stop the question sent by his eyes. Lana gazed back for long seconds before her lashes veiled the blue gleam in quick, flustered sweeps.

"If we will truly be wed, Aidan, and wed truly . . ." Her cheeks, already rosy, blazed red. "I would rather it be here beneath the trees." With trembling fingers, she drew his right hand from its arrest near her hip to the curve of one breast, first over the shift clinging there and then sliding between the hidden chemise and her skin. Her lips barely breathed the rest of her answer: "You needn't wait."

Her betrothed did not hear it. He fell into the sensations under his hand and back down against her to bury his face at her throat.

Aidan did not draw back or ask permission again. He could tell by her rising to him that he did not need to. He never completely forgot the pain that throbbed in his hand, nor the one that weighted his chest and muttered of violent deaths, but Lana helped him see beyond those to much better things. The wounds they both carried slipped off and lay beside them instead of crushing on top. Aidan drew Lana's eleven over his skin like a cloak, and inside it, found love. For a time, the humming of all other numbers dimmed behind the brilliant None they created in each other's arms.

The oaks, hazels, and yews of the grove heard that None, and they whispered.

AUTHOR'S NOTE

Although Aidan's story and the abbey of Saint Nevin are fictional, their backdrop is authentic. The witchcraft is based on ancient herbal lore, and life in the monastic society is compatible with the wide range of Irish practices at the time. Laymen first became involved in illumination around this era, too. Similarly, Aidan could not think of zero when he pondered the humming of None because the concept of a numeral zero would not appear in western cultures for several hundred years, and it wouldn't catch on until much later than that.

I have taken just a few conscious liberties with word choice or depictions, usually to remain within familiar paradigms and thus create more accurate pictures in readers' minds. Some cultural aspects of pre–Norman Christian Ireland, such as the frequent fostering of children, differed surprisingly from other western societies of the same era. To avoid tedious explanations, I did not address such customs when they seemed tangential to this story.

For readers troubled by such liberties or any unintentional errors, my apologies—with the caveat that fiction creates its own truth.